THE WORLD'S FINEST ASSASSIN

—— Gets Reincarnated in Another World as an Aristocrat ——

Contents

The World's Finest Assassin
Gets Reincarnated in Another World as an Aristocrat

† **Tarte**

Lugh's personal retainer and his assassination assistant. She cares deeply for Lugh because he saved her life.

† **Nevan**

A daughter of one of the four major dukedoms. She represents the peak of humanity.

† **Maha**

The proxy representative of Lugh's cosmetics brand. She provides logistical support by collecting funds, information, and more.

† **Lugh**

The oldest son of the clan of assassins, who is often called a boy genius. He was the world's greatest assassin in his previous life, and he combines that knowledge with the magic of his new world.

"...!"

† Alam Karla

The oracle of the Alamism religion. She can hear the voice of the goddess and is an object of worship for the people.

† Dia

Circumstances led to her becoming Lugh's little sister. She is among the strongest mages in the world.

THE
WORLD'S FINEST
ASSASSIN

Gets Reincarnated in Another World as an Aristocrat

6

Rui Tsukiyo

Illustration by Reia

YEN ON

New York

The World's Finest Assassin Gets Reincarnated in Another World as an Aristocrat, Vol. 6
Rui Tsukiyo

Translation by Luke Hutton
Cover art by Reia

SEKAI SAIKO NO ANSATSUSHA, ISEKAI KIZOKU NI TENSEI SURU Vol. 6
©Rui Tsukiyo, Reia 2021
First published in Japan in 2021 by KADOKAWA CORPORATION, Tokyo.
English translation rights arranged with KADOKAWA CORPORATION, Tokyo through TUTTLE-MORI AGENCY, INC., Tokyo.

English translation © 2022 by Yen Press, LLC

Yen On
150 West 30th Street, 19th Floor
New York, NY 10001

Visit us at yenpress.com
facebook.com/yenpress
twitter.com/yenpress
yenpress.tumblr.com
instagram.com/yenpress

First Yen On Edition: November 2022
Edited by Yen On Editorial: Jordan Blanco
Designed by Yen Press Design: Andy Swist

Yen On is an imprint of Yen Press, LLC.
The Yen On name and logo are trademarks of Yen Press, LLC.

Library of Congress Cataloging-in-Publication Data
Names: Tsukiyo, Rui, author. | Reia, 1990– illustrator.
Title: The world's finest assassin gets reincarnated in another world / Rui Tsukiyo ; illustration by Reia.
Other titles: Sekai saikou no ansatsusha, isekai kizoku ni tensei suru. English
Description: First Yen On edition. | New York : Yen On, 2020–
Identifiers: LCCN 2020043584 | ISBN 9781975312411 (v. 1 ; trade paperback) |
    ISBN 9781975312435 (v. 2 ; trade paperback) | ISBN 9781975333355 (v. 3 ; trade paperback) |
    ISBN 9781975334574 (v. 4 ; trade paperback) | ISBN 9781975334659 (v. 5 ; trade paperback) |
    ISBN 9781975343323 (v. 6 ; trade paperback)
Subjects: LCSH: Assassins—Fiction. | GSAFD: Fantasy fiction.
Classification: LCC PL876.S858 S4513 2020 | DDC 895.6/36—dc23
LC record available at https://lccn.loc.gov/2020043584

ISBNs: 978-1-9753-4332-3 (paperback)
        978-1-9753-4333-0 (ebook)

10 9 8 7 6 5 4 3 2 1

LSC-C

Printed in the United States of America

I had now encountered several demons: the orc demon, the beetle demon, the lion demon, the earth dragon demon, and the snake demon. Of these, the snake demon stood out from the rest.

She had disguised herself as a human and integrated into human society. This was not done solely out of a motivation to revive the Demon King, however. The snake demon enjoyed playing at being human because she had a fondness for our culture and pastimes. That interest was what gave me room to form an alliance with her. The information she gave me proved a tremendous boon, and I doubt we would've defeated the lion demon without her.

But now the first crack has formed in our accord.

The snake demon had elected not to tell me anything about the earth dragon demon. There was a chance she wasn't aware of everything her fellow demons did and was simply unaware of the earth dragon demon's activities. However, that became significantly less likely the moment Naoise appeared immediately after we defeated the earth dragon demon. She couldn't have arranged for her messenger to arrive at that time unless she knew about things beforehand.

Naoise was currently guiding us to the snake demon Mina's stronghold. I didn't feel like nonchalantly riding a giant serpent to her base of operations was the best idea, but there were answers that only Mina could provide. I was confident the girls and I could escape no matter what happened, and I'd also prepared some insurance. I wasn't so foolhardy as to charge into a demon's home without a plan.

Part of the reason I'd agreed to come along was because of Naoise. I was concerned about him.

"Are you sure you don't need to blindfold us, Naoise?" I asked. We were being taken to Mina's base, and I had to assume she didn't wish us to know its location. Typically, in scenarios like this, visitors would be blindfolded so they couldn't memorize the route.

"That's not an issue. You're Mistress Mina's ally, after all. And doing so would be pointless anyway," Naoise answered.

"You got me," I confessed with a small laugh. It was as Naoise said. Even if my vision had been obstructed, using wind magic to probe the surrounding area would have been a piece of cake.

"...Did Nevan not join you this time?"

"She's a busy person. She can't accompany us on every mission."

Nevan was a daughter of one of the four great dukedoms. She was also a masterwork—the product of generations of selective breeding to create perfect humans—and our upperclassman at the academy.

"Really? That's..." Naoise paused. He harbored affection for Nevan. I was curious if his next words would be "too bad" or "good," but he didn't continue.

"This snake is really fast," I remarked.

"And the ride is so smooth," said Tarte.

"It's slow compared to flying, though," Dia added.

Tarte's and Dia's beautiful gold and silver locks flowed in the wind despite their efforts to hold them down. As far as I could tell, we were traveling roughly three hundred kilometers per hour, a speed that rivaled the Shinkansen.

We continued at that rate through land untouched by man. There were plenty of forests yet to be cleared in this country, and many nobles were hard at work cultivating new regions.

We entered a large wood not on any map, and emerged in an unnaturally open area. The journey took about two hours. We alighted from the snake monster, and it burrowed underground and disappeared. It had served willingly as our taxi, but I imagined a monster of that caliber could easily lay waste to a small town.

"This is Mistress Mina's demon estate," announced Naoise.

The structure in question was massive and luxurious. Only high-ranking nobles could have built such a mansion. The rank of count would've been required, at the very least. Any lesser aristocrat with profitable businesses might have possessed the funds, but their peers would despise them for shooting above their station.

What caught my attention the most wasn't the size or the splendor, though.

"...This shouldn't be possible. The Nebia architectural style only just became popular in high society. And this building...was clearly designed by Nebia himself," I observed.

Nebia was a genius architect in this country, who had devised the estate of Count Chokorune. The architecture was so impressive that all aristocrats who visited the manor requested that Nebia remodel their homes. Eventually, nobles began to ask designers other than Nebia to mimic his style. It didn't take long for the architectural method to be named "Nebia," and it swiftly became the mainstream style in the Alvanian Kingdom.

It was too unbelievable that a demon had constructed a home of that fashion in such a remote location. Naoise looked at me and smiled.

"Your knowledge always impresses, Lugh. You're right, Nebia himself designed this estate. It was gifted to Mistress Mina by a noble admirer. He divided up his own mansion, then had it transported all the way out here and rebuilt."

"You make that sound simple. Only the most elite carpenters could pull off something like that. And there's no way Mina could take just anybody here."

"Mistress Mina is very popular."

"So that's how she did it."

The snake demon possessed the powerful ability to charm others. She'd likely brainwashed the necessary personnel and brought them to this place, all to build the manor she desired. Personally, I didn't hate Mina, but this was a good reminder that I was dealing with a genuine demon.

"Lugh, Dia, Tarte, please come with me. And welcome to my mistress's abode." Naoise opened the front door and ushered us inside.

So it was that we stepped into the snake's nest.

Within the mansion, there were many snake people in servant clothing going about their duties. They were hard at work cleaning, and they all bowed their heads when we drew near. Not only did Mina have a magnificent estate, she also kept the interior as clean and refined as any noble would. She even had exquisite works of art on display.

The upkeep on those pieces was flawless. Looking after high art demanded extremely specialized knowledge, and the monsters maintained Mina's collection perfectly. That struck me as strange. There were even lots of snake people behaving like knights, equipped with armor and swords and standing at attention. That felt off, too.

I could judge a knight's proficiency to an extent by examining their posture and gait. Unbelievably, Mina's dozens of soldiers all appeared to be elites. They possessed skill obtainable only after years of training that had to begin at a young age.

It should have been impossible. The concept of knighthood originated from humanity. There was no way monsters could be so familiar with its practices. Even if humans taught them, it had been less than a year since demons began reappearing. No one could master techniques in so short a time, monster or not.

...Hold on, that goes for the servants, too, I realized. Their etiquette was flawless, their skill at housework was top-notch, and they were maintaining art that necessitated specialized knowledge. They couldn't have learned all that overnight.

Even Tarte, as hard a worker as she was, needed years to reach her current skill level. The snake monsters were also acting way too human for my liking.

This all led me to a hypothesis that I didn't like very much. I would need to ask Mina about it.

Naoise led us to a guest room. The chamber's design was especially intricate, and the works of art were of even higher quality than those in the rest of the estate. The shelves were lined with bottles of alcohol, all luxurious items, both domestic and foreign. Each was a high-quality vintage from a prestigious and expensive brand. I wasn't particularly happy about it, but judging from this room, I could see that Mina's tastes aligned with mine.

The head of this manor was in the center of the room. "Welcome to my estate, Sir Lugh and his adorable lovers. I've been looking forward to hosting you for a very long time. Please, sit down," Mina greeted us.

She had dark skin and black hair. Her provocative clothing concealed very little of her voluptuous body, and her purple eyes resembled a serpent's. She was truly a woman of unmatched beauty.

"Your home is stunning, Mina. However, I can't say that I'm overjoyed with everything I've seen. In case you need a reminder, I am a human. It's in my nature to care for my fellow man," I responded sharply.

"Oh dear, I thought you might pick up on that," Mina replied with a suggestive smile. Dia and Tarte tilted their heads in confusion.

"You two saw the snake people working throughout the estate, right? They were created from humans. They're not monsters trained to become elite houseworkers and knights. It's the reverse. They're elite houseworkers and knights who were turned into monsters... Naoise told us earlier that Mina was gifted this mansion by a noble, but that isn't the whole truth. She was given the staff as well," I explained.

"What? That's horrible," Tarte responded.

"Oh, that makes sense. But that is *not* okay," said Dia.

Their faces went pale. They were both disgusted by what Mina had done. Anyone else would've felt the same.

"Please don't look at it that way. I didn't technically force any of them into it. They said they wanted to be with me forever, so I granted their wish. No harm has come to them. They're much stronger than humans now, and they are free from the concerns of aging," Mina protested.

"So charming others into obeying isn't compulsion to you? That's rich."

"My charm is part of my appeal. Complain all you want, but I can't help that. However, if I have offended you, then allow me to teach you about one of my abilities as an apology. I am able to eat living creatures and lay eggs. If I eat a person, I lay a snake person egg. Eating a dog gets me a snake dog, and eating a cat gets me a snake cat. They maintain their abilities and memories from their previous existences, and are reborn stronger than ever. It's a magnificent power, isn't it?"

"It's certainly a strong one."

It was repulsive, but I couldn't deny it was tremendously formidable. Mina was rapidly bewitching humans and making them into her playthings. Once she grew bored of them, she'd consume her toys and add them to her army. Mina had previously claimed she wasn't very strong for a demon, but having an army at her disposal would make her quite threatening.

"Oh, please don't give me that frightened look. You're going to awaken a fury of passion within me... I could just eat you up right now," Mina purred. She looked me up and down with her snake eyes, and Tarte and Dia stepped forward to protect me. "Please be at ease, adorable little lovers. I meant 'eat' in a sexual way."

"That hardly makes it better!" Tarte protested.

"Lugh isn't into old hags like you!" Dia spat.

Mina's face spasmed a little. Evidently, she didn't enjoy being called elderly.

"Anyway, let's sit. That's not what I came here to discuss. Am I correct in assuming you called us here to discuss a matter you can't speak of anywhere else?" I said.

"Yes. I am continually grateful for your sharp insight. I'll treat you to some alcohol. Which one would you like?"

"I'll have the Kurtonyu red."

Kurtonyu red wine, called the crimson jewel, was very rare and among the finest alcoholic beverages. Unfortunately, the special grapes used as an ingredient could no longer be harvested because the vineyard where they were grown was trampled by the orc demon's forces during the attack on the academy, meaning the wine was out of production. I chose it because I liked it, but also because of the irony.

"Oh goodness, that's my favorite. Did you know that people with similar tastes are said to be sexually compatible?"

"That's news to me."

Mina poured a cup of bloodred wine for all of us. So far, she had shown no signs of hostility. I couldn't let my guard down, though. One moment of carelessness could mean being devoured and turned into one of Mina's snake people. I had prepared insurance, but that didn't mean there wasn't any danger.

I would need to be careful as I talked to her.

So far, Mina and I had only traded jabs. This was where the real negotiation began.

I checked the wine to see if anything dangerous had been mixed into it. It would be safest to refrain from drinking it entirely, but my relationship with the snake demon was still amicable. I needed to at least pretend I trusted her.

There didn't seem to be any toxins. I signaled as much to Tarte and Dia with my eyes, and I took the first sip.

Kurtonyu red wine sure is good. Fine products like this were likely why Mina took a liking to human culture in the first place.

"Heh-heh, I've tried my fair share of human alcohol, and this is the most delicious," Mina commented.

"I agree," I responded. I swished the wine in my mouth. It had been preserved perfectly, retaining the striking taste of Kurtonyu.

After another sip, I eyed Mina. She smiled suggestively and waited for me to speak. It seemed I needed to get the ball rolling.

"I'll get right to the point. Do you intend to maintain our alliance?" I asked bluntly.

"Oh dear, where is this coming from?" Mina responded.

"Don't play dumb. I'm talking about the earth dragon. You surely noticed that it had been working to annihilate that town for some time. Yet you didn't contact me. I don't think it's a stretch to conclude that you wish to dissolve our agreement."

I wasn't going to let her evade the topic. I came here for the truth, no matter the consequences to our relationship.

"I elected not to tell you on purpose. I need a Fruit of Life. That little demon was powerful, but possessed a lethal weakness. Stealing the Fruit of Life after he produced it would've been simple. I didn't want you to get in the way."

"You hoped to take the Fruit of Life after the earth dragon demon created it."

"Precisely."

"...That doesn't make sense. If you need a Fruit of Life, why form a partnership with me? Your information allowed us to kill the lion demon before he could create what you need."

Mina paused to take a sip from her wine, then answered. "Frankly, I underestimated you. I didn't think you'd actually succeed when I gave you intel on the lion. At best, I thought you'd hold my irritating rivals back for a while. But now you've defeated four of us. Your latest opponent was the only demon left I believed I could successfully steal a Fruit of Life from. That's why I refrained from telling you."

"That makes sense."

"But I *still* failed. I never imagined you'd make it in time without my assistance. I'm also surprised you went head-to-head with that demon and won. You are truly strong, and, above all, you have a very discerning eye. You're the first human ever to notice that the earth dragon was nothing more than armor that weakling wore for protection."

A detail in Mina's words caught my interest. It was actually something I had been wondering about.

"The 'first,' you say. That means the earth dragon has fought humans before. Going back centuries, I presume. And I'm guessing that's true of the other demons, too. Are you all being repeatedly resurrected?"

I'd been studying all surviving literature on demons, and one thing repeatedly struck me as odd. No matter the era, the demons were always described like the ones of today, excluding some minor differences, despite the hero of each era slaying the demons.

How could the same demons keep appearing if the hero always killed them? Were the demons of the present and those of the past the same individuals? I'd been trying to work out that question for a while.

"We are resurrected. That word gives a slightly incorrect impression, though. After all, we don't die."

"You can die if your heart is shattered," I said. That was what Demonkiller was for, killing immortals.

"Having our hearts shattered renders us unable to remain in this world, but that is all. With time, we can manifest again."

Perhaps the process was similar to my own reincarnation. When humans were reborn, their souls were cleansed and bleached in the world after death. Then, they returned as new people. In my case, I skipped the cleansing and bleaching step and retained the memories of my previous life. It wouldn't have been astonishing to learn a similar thing happened with demons.

"That's very interesting. So you demons have been repeating the same process for centuries. You seem remarkably unprepared for the hero. Shouldn't you have formulated strategies by now? You've failed again and again, yet it still appears like you're relying on brute force. Surely demons are capable of learning."

In all of Alvan's recorded history, there was no mention of any great downfall of humanity. Thus, the demons and Demon King had to have lost every time. Why hadn't they concocted a plan against the hero by now?

"Since you know this much already, I may as well give you an important piece of information. We have never once failed. We have always achieved our goal, going back thousands of years. That is why the world still endures."

That sounded backward. Everyone knew that the demons and the Demon King sought to destroy the world, and the hero wanted to protect it. Mina's claim contradicted that.

"You're not going to explain in more detail, are you?" I questioned.

"Of course not. We're allies, not friends. I told you that as an apology for not informing you about the last demon. If you want more, I'll need compensation."

She was clearly suggesting I seek out the answer on my own. I wouldn't get the complete picture by looking into demons alone. I needed to meet with the hero.

"...Am I right in assuming you're willing to maintain our bargain?" I asked.

"Yes, that's right. Only four demons remain, including me. However, the other three are special. I can't do anything about them myself, so I'd be delighted if you took care of them."

"Do you expect me to trust what you say?"

"As I said before, I only withheld information to better my chances at getting a Fruit of Life. Do you see what I am getting at? If I get a Fruit of Life, we can return to the relationship we established... So may I please have that Fruit of Life you're hiding? If you don't give it to me, I'll have to dirty my hands and make one of my own. The other three remaining demons are too strong for me to steal from, so I'll have no other choice."

Mina's snake eyes moved to the Leather Crane Bag hanging from my hip. Playing dumb wasn't an option. I was also certain she could create a Fruit of Life if she so desired. This woman had the Alvanian Kingdom practically dancing on the palm of her hand. Her political influence was enough to keep me away while she slaughtered innocents in some town beyond my reach.

That gave me only one choice.

"I accept your terms, if we do this the other way around. Continue to give me intel on demons. When you're the last one left, I'll give the fruit to you."

That would keep Mina in check and allow us to maintain our alliance. Anger flashed across the snake demon's face for a moment, and then it swiftly returned to her usual beguiling expression.

"You're a very cautious man."

"I'm giving you a penalty. You reneged on our agreement, so you should be the one saddled with disadvantageous terms, not me."

"I hope you don't forget your lives are at stake in this negotiation. This is my nest, and you're exhausted from your previous fight."

Mina was correct on both accounts. There were hundreds of powerful monsters in this mansion. I'd also used all of my Fahr Stones and lost my cannons in the battle against the earth dragon. My mana and stamina had returned, thanks to Rapid Recovery, but we would stand little chance in a battle here.

"And I would think you know better. I knew full well we'd be imperiled the moment we stepped foot in your base. Do you really think me careless enough to come here without a plan in case things went wrong? I not gambling our lives. Want to try me?"

I locked eyes with Mina. We both excelled at reading the intentions of others. That was how we were able to come to an understanding.

"You win. I accept your terms. I'll offer you more information about my fellow demons, and I'll support you with my political influence as well. If you're uncomfortable with me eating humans, I'll refrain from that, too. In exchange, you'll give me the Fruit of Life when I'm the last demon remaining, as you promised."

"We have a deal. All right, we're done here. Tarte, Dia, let's return home."

"Y-yes, my lord," replied Tarte.

"Yeah, I don't wanna spend more time here than we have to," said Dia.

I stood, and they followed suit. They both wore stiff expressions; the strange mood in this room must have made them nervous.

"...I have two final warnings for you, Sir Lugh. First, I recommend you don't carry the Fruit of Life around for very long. It's fodder for the Demon King, and too much for a human to handle. You're not a monster like the hero, don't forget that. You're merely a stronger person. Second, you need to decide what it is you want to protect. Is it the world, this country, or your adorable little lovers? You'll make the wrong decision if you're not careful. This ritual is reaching its climax, and you'll have to make a decision soon. It's already been perverted by the presence of a lowly human. Even I don't know what is going to happen."

"Thanks, I'll keep that in mind. What do you want in exchange?"

"That was just a gift to my favorite boy. If you really want to thank me, how about you do so in bed?"

"I'm going to have to decline. Sorry, but you're not my type."

"Oh, how cold. Though I have to admit, I like that side of you."

Nothing was surprising about Mina's first warning; I figured the Fruit of Life was dangerous. And from what I'd learned so far, I could guess why she chose this time to ask me what I wanted to protect.

There was no way I would ever waver in regard to that question. I'd been reborn with the aim to live as a person, not a tool. My purpose in life as Lugh Tuatha Dé was to live happily with the people I loved. That was all.

We left Mina's estate. The snake demon and Naoise were seeing us off. They asked if we wanted to have the snake carry us back, but I politely refused. If anyone witnessed me riding that giant snake, I would be ruined.

I wanted to talk to Naoise alone before we left, but I guess that's not going to happen. Now that I thought about it, though, that would have been pointless. Even if I got him by himself, unattended, he would just tell his mistress everything I said.

Knowing that, I came to a decision. I would speak my mind, even if it meant Mina learned of it.

"Naoise, tell me something. Why are you here?"

I wanted to know if Naoise was still himself. If he claimed he was here for Mina, then I'd know that the true Naoise was gone and that only a puppet remained.

Naoise opened his mouth robotically.

He's gone, isn't he...? Actually, wait.

The young man's face twisted into the expression of one who was working desperately to protect all that was important to him. It was a very human look. He spoke as if forcing the words out. "I'm here to...become stronger. When I am, I'll..." The rest of what he said was drowned out by the wind, but that was enough. I knew Naoise was okay.

"I see. Until next time, Naoise."

Despite the danger, I'd been considering tearing him away from Mina had he lost himself. Trying to force him away from her now would likely cause him to perceive me as an enemy and attack. Even if I did manage to force him to come home, he'd immediately return to the demon. A plan like that threatened to break Naoise for good. In such a scenario, I'd have no recourse but to attempt a heavy-handed method with a slim chance of success to restore my lost friend's humanity.

Fortunately, though, he was still himself. There was no need to take the gamble. I could leave him here.

"Until next time, Lugh. We'll most likely see each other next at the academy," Naoise responded.

I looked at Mina. She smiled and said nothing. The academy's reconstruction was going well, and students would be called back before long. Did Mina intend to send Naoise in his present state?

"Got it. See you at the academy, then."

That was fine by me. I didn't know what the demon had planned, but if she was going to give me time with Naoise away from her, I would use it to heal him, even if it was a trap.

I relied on my memory of the path to Mina's estate to fly to the nearest town, and then rented a room at an inn. Alvan was a relatively safe country, but this town was an exception; it was straight up dangerous.

I chose the best lodgings available out of safety concerns. The cost per room here was determined by comfort, sanitation, and safety. To stay at a cheap inn was to risk your life. You were lucky if all that happened was someone drugging your food with sleep medicine and stealing your possessions. People were bought and sold as commodities in this town.

I collapsed on the bed as soon as I entered the room. Dia followed suit and lay down next to me.

"Today was exhausting," I said.

Dia nodded. "Yeah, I'm pooped."

"It is rare for you to show such open fatigue, my lord," Tarte observed.

"What about me?" Dia asked defensively.

"Um, this is nothing out of the ordinary for you," Tarte answered honestly, though she averted her eyes.

"I had to work all the time to keep up appearances when I lived as a high-born girl in Viekone. Trying to act so tough all the time just started to feel really stupid when I began living with Lugh."

Dia was still able to hide all weakness flawlessly when she needed to conduct herself as a noble. However, she allowed her true personality to emerge around me, Tarte, and others she trusted.

"I'm exhausted, too. I have recovered physically, but not mentally," Tarte confessed.

"Yeah, Rapid Recovery is *super* useful. You can push yourself as hard as you like, and get your stamina back immediately... My mind is still fried," Dia remarked.

That was the biggest weakness of Rapid Recovery—it only aided the body. Even *my* mind was in tatters after the close-call battle with the earth dragon and meeting with Mina for negotiations. That's why I decided to rest in a nearby town rather than push myself to return to Tuatha Dé immediately.

"Oh yeah, are you back to normal yet, Tarte?" Dia questioned. "You always end up causing trouble after using Beastification for an extended amount of time."

Tarte blushed. She was very sensitive about how lustful the side effects of Beastification made her. "I've been transforming for a little bit every day to get used to it as Lord Lugh instructed, so I'm able to restrain myself now."

She said "restrain." That meant the impulse was likely still there. Her eyes did look slightly impassioned.

"Okay, so you can hold out," Dia said.

"Um, is something wrong?" Tarte asked.

Shaking her head, Dia replied, "Nope, it's nothing. Anyway, let's eat. I'm starving."

"Me too. I wonder if Rapid Recovery causes you to get hungry faster, in addition to the speedy recuperation. Carrying around my heavy spear all day hasn't helped, either."

Tarte glanced at the magic spear that was propped against the wall. I usually stored it in the Leather Crane Bag, but I didn't know how the Fruit of Life might affect it. Carrying it while hang gliding must have been difficult, and Tarte had garnered odd looks in town for lugging a giant mechanical weapon on her back.

Not being able to use my Leather Crane Bag was a huge inconvenience. I would need to free it up again when I returned to Tuatha Dé.

Dinner was okay.

"Ugh, the bread and alcohol aren't great," groaned Dia.

"They are very...plain," Tarte agreed.

This town's food couldn't match the luxury of the royal capital, the worldwide variety of Milteu, or the freshness of Tuatha Dé. We had all developed discriminating palates, and weren't entirely satisfied by the food we were served. It didn't help that the prices were about the same as were found at inns in the royal capital. We were paying for safety more than anything else here.

"At least they make up for the taste with quantity. If I had to guess, I'd say this is a pub aimed at blue-collar workers," I stated. Certain exceptions aside, upper-class people would never come to this town.

The day's massive main dish of fried pork arrived. Judging it by appearances alone, I'd say it looked incredible. They used all parts of the pig—I saw boneless rib, sirloin, liver, heart, small intestine, and more—and everything was thoroughly cooked and lathered in salty-sweet sauce.

The meat had been fried for too long, likely to make up for the lack of freshness. There was a stench that the sauce was unable to completely mask, but the meat was edible, if only just.

Surprisingly, the taste was acceptable. There was a fair variety to the selections, and the relatively strong flavoring went well with alcohol.

"Well, it's easier to get down than I'd anticipated," I said.

"This is more than satisfactory for me," Tarte claimed.

"Meals like this are good every now and then, too," added Dia.

We always ate home cooking in Tuatha Dé, but Mom and I both liked to prepare elegant meals. Without this kind of establishment, we probably would never have gotten to eat such rustic food.

I was back in my room taking care of a tedious task when Dia peeked over my shoulder. We'd rented two bedchambers, one for me and one for the girls, but they were hanging out in mine in their pajamas. Their nightwear was thin and alluring.

Dia had been noticeably growing lately and was looking more like a woman each day. I thought she might end up bigger than my mother.

"What are you doing?" she asked.

"I'm writing today's report. I need to make sure I send it... I want to leave out the fact that we killed another demon, but unfortunately, that's not an option," I answered.

The news of our triumph over another demon was going to cause great excitement in the kingdom. We'd now killed half of them. The whole country would believe we'd triumph over all the demons, and they'd worship us for it. I wanted to avoid that, but the earth dragon's statue in the Sanctuary had surely broken by now, so hiding our deed was impossible.

"Why? I'm sure you'll receive another medal and more money. You might even receive new territory and gain a higher title."

"I don't want a higher title. If my territory gets any larger, I won't be able to keep track of it all, and I'd probably get roped into the politics of the central government. Being a baron suits me best."

Nobles acquired greater authority and wealth as they rose higher in the ranks. However, with each advancement came more duties. Barons were mostly fine to focus on their own domain. If I moved up in society, I'd be forced to participate in politics whether I wanted to or not, and I would also need to watch over lower-ranking nobles. It'd be way too much of a pain.

Lesser aristocrats did have to deal with occasional outrageous commands from superiors, but even then, a promotion wasn't worth it.

"You really have no ambition," Dia commented.

"I do. I will obtain everything I desire, everything I need to bring happiness to myself and the people I love. None of that necessitates a higher rank, though."

There were few things I couldn't already acquire in my current position. Conversely, a higher title would only bring me troubles I wanted no part of.

"Heh, you're right. I'd much rather spend time with you as I please than see you rise in society. Father was always crazy busy, and we rarely had time to eat together."

"He's a count, so that's not surprising... It might be best for me to make my intentions clear to the rest of the aristocracy. Maybe that will prevent any more nobles from trying to bring me down out of envy like Marquis Carnalie."

"You mean you're going to publicly declare that you don't want a higher rank?"

"That would be the fastest method, but it would also bring its own host of annoying characters."

Human hearts were irrational and complicated. Understanding one or two people was one thing, but any more than that was hopeless.

"All right, I'm done with the letter. All that remains is to send it first thing in the morning. I'm going to sleep early. I'm studying the Fruit of Life tomorrow, so I need to rest up."

"...Oh, that's disappointing," Dia said before embracing me from behind. Her body temperature felt hotter than usual. Her intentions were clear.

"Aren't you tired?" I asked.

"I'm exhausted, but I'm in the mood. My switch gets flipped on whenever I think I might lose you. You put yourself in such danger during the fight with the demon earlier, and you felt so distant when you talked to Mina. You were like an entirely different person. I've felt this way all day. I checked to see if Tarte was in the mood for sex earlier because I decided I would have to give you up if she couldn't endure her side effects. I'm being weird, aren't I?"

"I don't think so. I know how you feel," I answered, hoping to clear Dia's anxiety. I wanted to set her mind at ease through our mutual touch. I wanted to feel her as well. Dia also simply looked too adorable as she abashedly confessed her feelings, and I was unable to resist.

"Eek!"

Like magic, I freed myself from Dia's embrace, picked her up, and then carried her to the bed. Dia peered at me with moist eyes, and spread her arms wide to invite me in.

"I'm not going anywhere," I assured her.

"Yeah, I trust you," she responded.

I smiled and kissed her.

I was here, and I would never leave Dia's side. I was going to ensure she knew that.

We were eating breakfast at the inn. I didn't have high expectations for the food, but it wasn't bad. They had obviously considered nutrition, and it was adequately filling.

"Hmm-hmm-hmm."

Dia was humming cheerfully, most likely because of our love-making session last night. She didn't get in that kind of mood very often, but once that switch was flipped, she always gave herself over to me completely.

Tarte watched with clear jealousy. Dia and I hadn't told her about what we did last night, but she had caught on somehow.

"Um, are we returning home after this?" Tarte inquired.

"As soon as I send my letter," I answered.

I was very anxious about the Fruit of Life. Worst case scenario it could break my Leather Crane Bag from the inside, so I couldn't put off studying it much longer. The Leather Crane Bag was valuable to me, and replacing it would be extremely difficult. I didn't want to use it if possible, but I had no other safe means of storing and carrying the Fruit of Life. I did cover the Fruit of Life with a special alloy, but I didn't know how much that would actually accomplish.

"Wanna buy some souvenirs?" Dia proposed. "I think it's important to do nice things for your parents once in a while."

"In this town? I don't recommend it... How about we look at some street stalls on the way to dropping off my letter? That should give you enough of a chance to find something," I responded.

"Sounds good. If I don't see anything I like, I won't force myself to make a purchase!"

Our plans were made, and we were done eating. It was time to depart.

We walked down the main street, heading for the post office. As evidenced by our passable accommodations being considered the best lodgings in town, this settlement was unsafe. To paint a picture of how bad public order was, a woman walking alone in public might as well have been putting herself on display in a brothel. If one was naive enough to think they could walk the streets unaccompanied, that would be it for them.

I'd met the ruler of this domain before, and he wasn't exactly one to live by societal rules. The policies here were loose, a reflection of his character. No one who came here was rejected, whether they be criminal or foreigner or whatever else. Laws didn't really exist, either. Everything that happened to you was your responsibility. If you were robbed, beaten, or worse, all you could do was cry yourself to sleep.

A decent person would never come to this town. The population was made up almost entirely of those with nowhere else to go, or the sort with businesses that were illegal in other places. Illicit goods were easily procured here, and ill-gotten gains served as the primary industry.

Simply put, this town was trouble, and we witnessed that

firsthand in the form of the incessant pests that approached Dia and Tarte as we strolled. I was sure each had their individual motives, but they all knew that two beautiful young girls would fetch them a great sum, and no one would blame them for kidnapping Dia and Tarte.

Even people were commodities in this town. Beautiful young girls sold well. To these pests, abducting people and hawking them felt no different than picking up money left on the street.

"You're showing these people no mercy, my lord," said Tarte.

"Whoa, you sent him flying, too. Look at that parabola," remarked Dia.

"They leave me no other choice," I explained.

Dealing with every one of the disgusting men who approached us would be exhausting, so I decided to knock each of them out with a wind uppercut to the jaw before they could get a word out. Dia and Tarte were more than strong enough to protect themselves, but the carnal lust of these men seemed to frighten them, and they clung to me for protection. The pests were guilty in my eyes the moment they scared Dia and Tarte, and I was going to make each of them pay.

Dia came to a stop a little farther down the street.

"Wow, that's a beautiful necklace. The gem is really nice, and the craftsmanship is exquisite. It's so cheap, too. The price could easily be three times more expensive. Should I buy this for Mother?"

The "Mother" she was referring to was mine. Dia and I were pretending to be siblings, so she called her that in public to ensure our cover wasn't blown.

I followed Dia's gaze and saw a perfectly ordinary stall selling a necklace that was nice enough to impress her elite sense of aesthetics. Not only was it fine enough to be worn among high society without any shame, it was liable to garner admiration from other aristocrats. It was that luxurious of an item.

"You should forget about it," I warned her.

"Huh? I promise you this is genuine. I'll prove it to you if you don't believe me," Dia objected.

"That price on an item of that caliber means it's dangerous— stolen. Remember what I told you about this town?"

"Oh, yeah… You're right. Anyone with a trained eye would know the necklace's origin at a glance."

There wasn't much mass production in this era, especially when it came to finery. Almost all high-quality items were unique works made by famed artisans. As such, wearing stolen jewelry in high society would mean swift discovery, and you'd be made a laughingstock. Word spread quickly between nobles.

Normally, stolen jewelry would be broken up and sold in pieces. However, while this necklace did use a nice gem, its value came from its exquisite design and superior craftsmanship, so taking it apart would significantly reduce its value. That was why it was left whole and put up for sale at a discount price.

The only people who'd buy that necklace were those in a position where it didn't matter if they wore pilfered goods, or the few who desired such pieces for private collections.

A balance was struck in this stolen valuables market between thieves who desired safe exchange of illicit items and consumers after quality items for cheap. An example of the latter would be a noble from a remote, rural region. The risk of people discovering that they wore swiped trinkets was low, so they could go peruse a market like this with impunity.

"Well, that sucks. I thought it would be nice for Mother to have at least one nice piece of jewelry to wear," Dia lamented.

"Mom just isn't into that stuff," I responded.

House Tuatha Dé held the lowly rank of baron, but thanks to our medical technology and secret assassin operation, we earned significantly more than most viscounts. We could live in luxury if we so desired, but my mom wasn't interested in that.

"That's exactly why I wanted it. She'll never dress up unless someone pushes her to, so I thought this was a good opportunity. I know it'd make her happy if it was a present from you," Dia explained.

She was probably right. Mom didn't care about draping herself in expensive things, but other nobles mocked her for not doing so. I wanted to stick it to those idiots.

"...Okay. I'll ask Maha to send me some nice gemstones from Milteu. Mom would probably feel guilty and refuse a necklace I bought, but she'll happily wear something I make." Having reached my decision, I promptly walked away from the stall.

"You're not going to buy one here? Look at how cheap these jewels are," said Dia.

"I suppose I could. No one would realize the gems were stolen, and it would be cheaper. However, I don't like the idea of Mom wearing something purchased here. And most importantly, I'm going to make our engagement ring, too. I'm sure you wouldn't like that to be crafted from stolen materials," I responded.

"Y-yeah, you're right. Wait, what did you just say?! Engagement ring?! How could you be so casual about that?! You've never mentioned a ring!" Dia exclaimed.

"We were on the topic of jewelry, and after watching all these men approach you, it occurred to me that an engagement ring would serve as a nice deterrent to keep their kind away. I actually planned on making it sooner, but we've been so busy that it slipped my mind."

Dia and I were engaged. Siblings getting married wasn't rare in Alvan, so there was no need to hide it. On the contrary, the ring would be a convenient way to ward off unwanted men.

"...I'm so happy. My heart is racing just thinking of having a symbol of our engagement." Dia took the hem of my jacket with her eyes cast down.

"I'm going to make you a really great one. I'm sure you'll love it."

This was going to be our engagement ring—I had to make it special. I was going to fixate on every aspect, down to the materials incorporated. I would also use the giant network of my company, Natural You, to obtain items of the highest quality.

I figured I might as well give the ring offensive magic capabilities while I was at it. Fahr Stones could store magic, but there were gems capable of retaining mana as well, and they could even be engraved with formulas.

Congratulations, Lady Dia." Tarte smiled, yet there was a slight trace of sadness and jealousy in her expression that only an expert like me could have noticed.

I gave a strained grin and patted her on the head. "Don't act like you're not a part of this. I'm going to make you one, too, of course."

Tarte put her hands over her mouth and looked up at me. Tears began to streak down her face. "U-um, well, that would make me very, very happy, but I'm a servant, and a commoner... I-is that going to be okay?" she asked timidly.

"Of course. Or do you not want to marry me?" I replied.

"Of course I do!!" she practically shouted.

Wow, that was kind of scary. Tarte looked like a child who thought her toy would be taken away.

"That side of you is simultaneously annoying and adorable, Tarte," Dia teased.

"Yeah, sure is," I agreed.

Pouting, Tarte responded, "Ohhhh, you two are so mean."

The three of us laughed together. Dia and Tarte were adorable and very special to me. I would do anything for them.

I delivered my report to the royal capital using a carrier pigeon. Once that was done, the three of us returned to the Tuatha Dé estate. I then used a telecommunications device in the domain to call Maha and inform her of my budget and the gemstones that I wanted. With that done, I headed to the mountain behind my family's manor.

Tuatha Dé citizens were prohibited from entering this place, and I'd instructed Tarte and Dia not to come near me no matter what happened, too. That meant that whatever transpired, I'd be the only one hurt.

"I don't know what awaits me with this thing, but it's not gonna be good…"

It was finally time to take the Fruit of Life out of the Leather Crane Bag. Anticipation and fear swirled in my gut. This was the power to summon the Demon King. Who could say how great it was?

This is unbelievable...

I stood astonished as I beheld the raw power of the Fruit of Life. I'd expected it to be massive beyond my estimations, of course, but it exceeded even the realm of imagination.

The Fruit of Life was more than a mass of energy. The over ten thousand souls weren't just consumed and converted into nourishment, they were reborn as a single fruit. It had a pulse, and it was alive.

That set its very essence apart from Fahr Stones, which were no more than mana batteries. The Fruit of Life, however, was a generator that produced an endless amount of mana. Many things could store magical power, but only life created it.

The Demon King was born after eating several of these. I got chills just thinking about it. A single Fruit of Life was so powerful that I thought it might rival Epona's might. If the Demon King was formed using multiple Fruits of Life and demons, he would be invincible.

More immediately troubling was the saliva that had been building in my mouth. Just like the first time I saw this incredible object, a craving was raging in my chest.

I want to eat it. It looks delicious. I had never felt such hunger before. I once fasted for two weeks for training purposes, and the desire I felt then paled in comparison.

My instincts were screaming for me to eat the fruit. It was such a sweet temptation. I felt like I would lose my mind if I didn't bite into it at once.

Fortunately, my reason triumphed. There was no way I could handle such massive power. The nature of the fruit was what made it so dangerous. If it had been no more than a pure mass of energy, I would have been able to adapt using Rapid Recovery and Limitless Growth. I could eat it bit by bit, heal any damage to my body as I went, and adjust to the new strength. It would be possible for me.

However, this power was alive. I would cease to be myself. It was an unnatural, overwhelming thing made by forcibly bundling and blending the wishes and emotions of over ten thousand people. If I consumed all that, assuming I survived, Lugh Tuatha Dé would vanish, and I would become some other entity. Only a puppet of the Fruit of Life would remain.

This is a literal forbidden fruit. I smiled painfully. There was no doubt I would become very strong if I ate it. I would become a monster that surpassed the hero. In exchange, I would lose everything that made me who I was.

Sometimes it was important to follow your instincts, but this was not such an occasion. I overcame the compulsion with reason, and pushed aside dark temptation.

To an assassin, a cool mind was the greatest weapon.

"Okay, time to see your true colors."

I overcame all emotions and instincts and began to analyze the violent crystallization of human souls. Undoubtedly, understanding its true nature would reveal some hidden secrets.

Five hours later, I'd managed to drag myself back to the estate.

"*Aaaah!* What happened to you, my lord?!" Tarte screamed, dropping the plates she was carrying.

"I overdid it...just a little. Don't worry... I performed...first aid. Call Dad for me... I can't heal myself...any further..."

I was in horrific condition. My clothes were tattered and drenched with blood, and there was a large laceration in my chest. My left hand was horribly burned, my right arm was broken, and my ribs and my left leg were cracked. I hadn't been wounded this badly in a long time.

To make matters worse, mana containing the Fruit of Life's will surrounded my body, obstructing the effects of Rapid Recovery. Fortunately, I'd avoided injuries that would leave permanent after-effects.

"Understood! I will call for Lord Tuatha Dé immediately!"

"Thanks. I'll be waiting in my room."

Dad was the best doctor in the country. I was in good hands.

I'd hit my limit. I leaned on the wall, all but collapsing against it. Tarte sprinted to Dad's study. I walked to my room as best as I could.

"I was carrying around an outrageously powerful bomb..."

My body was ragged, and I was all out of mana. Despite that, the corners of my mouth twisted into a smile. Although my injuries were grievous, I'd made some tremendous discoveries. Despite the difficulty, I'd successfully analyzed the Fruit of Life.

I'd gained new strength in the process and learned a rule that the goddess, the demons, and the church had been concealing. That was significantly more valuable than mere strength.

I discovered an option the goddess and the demons had kept to themselves. If I picked it, I could aim for a conclusion that neither the goddess nor the demons—the players of this game—desired. And I intended to do just that. Following the guidelines they'd set would lead to my happiness crumbling.

I get it now.

I finally understood why Epona would go mad in the future.

I opened my eyes. My body had been healed, and my clothes changed to comfortable pajamas. Bandages covered me, and while I didn't know how it'd been accomplished, the harmful mana blocking my recovery was gone.

Dad really was the best. He'd treated me flawlessly.

"Ah, you're awake, my lord!"

"You have no idea how much you worried me, Lugh."

Tarte and Dia took my hands and spoke to me as soon as they saw that I was awake.

"...I lost consciousness," I remarked.

"You gave me a shock. When I led Lord Tuatha Dé to your room, we found you collapsed motionless in front of your bed," Tarte explained.

Tearfully, Dia admitted, "I thought you were dead for a second."

I remembered it faintly. When I entered my bedchamber, all of my strength finally left me and I tumbled to the floor.

"Sorry about that. I pushed myself too far this time," I apologized.

"Take us with you if you're going to do something that risky!" Dia scolded.

"Yes, please do! It's my duty to protect you, my lord!" Tarte added.

"It was too risky. One mistake and I would've died. If you two had been there, you absolutely would've been injured…and significantly worse than me," I responded. Put bluntly, the Fruit of Life's power was absolutely too much for me to handle.

"That's *why* we needed to be there. We've gotten stronger, too. We don't need you to guard us all the time, Lugh," Dia protested.

"That's right. I'm working hard every day to hone the power you gave me," Tarte said.

Ever since I gave them Rapid Recovery and Limitless Growth using My Loyal Knights, the girls had been performing additional training to improve their physical capabilities and increase their mana capacities. The results were beginning to show, and Dia and Tarte now stood at the peak of human capability.

I only needed to reflect on our battles against the demons to understand that they were right. I wouldn't have defeated any of the demons on my own. I'd only been able to kill those monsters because Dia and Tarte were with me. They didn't need me to shield them anymore… I should have understood that.

"You're right. I'll ask for your help next time." There was nothing for me to do but agree. I had to acknowledge Dia and Tarte as ready.

"I'm glad you can admit your mistake. I'm going back to my room. Take today to rest, okay?" Dia urged.

"Will do. I am pretty tired." Rapid Recovery had restored a

significant portion of my stamina and mana already, yet my body felt like lead, and it was difficult to think straight.

Fidgeting, Tarte asked, "Um, can you eat? Lord Tuatha Dé said you were well enough to."

"Then I'll try. Something light like noodles would be nice," I requested.

"Yes, my lord. I'll get right on it."

As the two left the room, I sat up and called, "Hey, am I still me?"

"What kind of question is that? Of course you're you," Dia answered.

"Um, are you not feeling well?!" Tarte questioned with clear urgency.

"No, it's nothing. Sorry for the weird question." I lay back down in the bed.

I'd had an accident when I was analyzing the Fruit of Life. I was very curious to study it, but I never intended to use it for power. Attempting to do so would have been too dangerous.

However, I underestimated what it meant for the Fruit of Life to be alive and possess a will of its own. It acted toward goals; that's why it tempted me to eat it. I thought I was safe when I resisted that urge, but that's when the fruit played its next card. *It* tried to consume *me*.

The Fruit of Life formed a connection with me. The collective consciousness of over ten thousand souls crushed my individuality, and I was pushed to the brink of becoming a puppet for fulfilling the fruit's goal. Fortunately, I used the insurance I'd prepared just in time, and I managed to protect myself while quieting the connection.

I learned a lot when the Fruit of Life took hold of me, for it filled my head with its goal and how to achieve it. That came with a consequence, though—I was still connected to it. I'd weakened the link, but I wasn't able to sever it.

"...Hahhh... What should I do about this?"

I lifted a hand, and a vast amount of mana flowed from it. The amount was several times greater than what I could release with my instantaneous mana discharge. Undoubtedly, the source of this energy was the Fruit of Life, which I'd sealed in the Tuatha Dé domain using a secret method. Still, no matter the distance, I was linked to the fruit, and reaching out to it a little was all it took to produce this much mana. The output would be far greater if I unleashed its full power.

I only intended to use it in dire situations. This power was a double-edged sword. If anything went wrong, I could cease to be me; it was that dangerous. That said, this strength was undeniably great. If I was to follow the path that enabled me to outmaneuver the goddess and the demons, I undoubtedly wouldn't require this incredible might.

I needed to think of a way to live with it safely, even if that was playing into the Fruit of Life's plan.

It was the third morning since the day I was so heavily injured. My body felt light, and the pain was gone.

"I've finally recovered."

The wounds I'd suffered while examining the Fruit of Life had healed without so much as a lingering trace. I had my dad's precise medical treatment to thank for that. If I'd left the rehabilitation to my accelerated self-healing from Rapid Recovery, there surely would've been scars.

An assassin's appearance was very important. A good first impression is pivotal to getting near your target, and for better or worse, appearance plays a significant role in that. Horrific scars or burns would be a major handicap.

"I would have been bedridden for a year if I didn't have Rapid Recovery."

My injuries were so bad my body needed three days to heal. Rapid Recovery initially increased my recuperation by a hundredfold, and I had raised the proficiency of the skill to multiply the ratio by dozens more times than that. It took a lot to render me bedridden for so long.

"I've somehow gotten used to that new power, too..."

The small piece of the Fruit of Life's power that penetrated my body had become part of my flesh and blood. I had put a lid over the energy, but I could feel the connection distinctly.

At present, it only worked in my favor, but I couldn't be careless. I was carrying around a bomb and needed to find a way to live with it safely.

I used the messaging function of my communications device to see if there had been any important messages in the last three days. There was only one, and it was from Maha. Tarte had told her about my condition, and she wanted me to call her when I woke up.

I did so immediately. I doubted she would be able to answer because of how busy she was, so I was going to leave a message telling her when I would be free to talk. I was surprised, however, when she picked up instantly. She must have been hovering over the communications device, waiting for me to call.

"How are you feeling?!"

"I'm fine. I feel stronger than ever before, in fact."

"Thank goodness, I was so worried. I considered abandoning my work and racing to you more than a few times."

"Why didn't you?"

"Because this is the battlefield you left me, dear brother."

"You're a good girl."

Maha always did what needed to be done. There were few people who could consistently follow through on that like she did. I was also very grateful that she had subordinates she could trust to take over her work in times of emergency. I could rely on her for anything.

"You must know I don't like being spoken to like I'm a child."

"Sorry. I can't seem to break the habit. Is that all you needed?"

"No. I've obtained the materials you wanted for the necklace and rings you're making. As you requested, I got diamond, emerald, sapphire, alexandrite, and mithril, too."

"I appreciate it."

"I wanted to get AAA grade for all of them, but I was only able to manage AA for the emerald, sapphire, and alexandrite. I apologize."

"Actually, I'd rather have AA for all of them but the diamond."

The AAA grade was bestowed to less than 3 percent of all jewels. I gave Maha this request on short notice, so it was understandable that she couldn't do better. Also, I knew of techniques to turn AA gems into AAA ones.

"Hey, can I ask you a question?"

"Sure."

"I know the necklace is a present for Lady Esri, and you also told me you're making engagement rings... But why do you need three stones for the rings? Will one have two gems? I've never heard of such a design."

There was both anxiety and hope in Maha's voice. I knew what she wanted to hear.

"No, I'm just making three rings. Diamonds project both strength and elegance through their radiance, their variety of cuts give them a great range of expression, and their nature as the hardest mineral reminds one of an ironclad will. That fits Dia's personality perfectly. The diamond is for her."

"That's not how I think of diamonds. They do possess

a unique shine, but they're mostly used in manufacturing because of their hardness. They're not valued highly on the market among other gemstones."

"That's why I said diamonds can express many different things depending on the cut."

This world lacked the knowledge of how to refine diamonds. Diamonds are incredibly hard, which made them difficult to process. They weren't particularly beautiful when raw, either.

Diamonds had been valued as lowly stones in my previous world until technology advanced to the point that cutting them became feasible. As Maha said, their primary use was in manufacturing.

I, however, knew how to shape diamonds to make them beautiful. I would create one more beautiful than any other gemstone, a worthy gift for Dia.

"I'd like to see the finished product. What about the other gemstones?"

"The emerald fits Tarte's personality. Its jade-green color gives it a warm brilliance, and its simple presence is calming. That is who Tarte is to me."

Emeralds weren't just beautiful; they had a healing effect on the heart.

"That does sound like Tarte. She's relaxing to be around... So what about the sapphire?" Maha's voice shook. She seemed really nervous. It was time to stop messing with her.

"The sapphire is a beautiful blue gemstone that projects placidity and intelligence. Its shine engenders a shimmering and alluring charm. You're always so serene, and smarter than anybody I know. The sapphire suits you perfectly. I wanted this to be a surprise for the next time we met, but after you asked, I felt I had to tell you."

I heard a gasp. Maha didn't respond for some time. She must have been fighting hard to contain her emotions.

"...Um, thank you. I'll look forward to the completed ring."

"I'll make you one of the greatest rings this world has seen. Changing the subject, can you come out here in the next week or so? I think it's about time I introduce you to my parents. We're getting engaged, so that's a must. I'll give you your ring then."

"I'll find a way to make it work. How long is a round trip by carriage? Adjusting my schedule is going to be difficult."

"I'll come get you with an aircraft. I can get you here and back in a day, so that's all the time you'll need to free up."

"In that case, I can definitely make it work. I'll be there!"

"I'm looking forward to it. We'll hammer down the date during our next call."

I ended the transmission. Maha had successfully acquired all the jewels I'd asked for.

"I should get to work on the designs." I headed to my desk.

I'd played the part of an art dealer or a designer several times to get close to assassination targets, so I had plenty of knowledge and skill when it came to designing jewelry. I was going to make accessories that brought out the unique charm of each woman in my life.

One week later, the gemstones and mithril I'd requested arrived together with my mother's regular Natural You shipment. I quickly took them to a workshop I'd built.

"I don't think watching me make jewelry is going to be very interesting, you two," I said.

"I've been *dying* to watch your technique!" Dia responded.

"Yes, I'm excited as well," Tarte agreed.

They said they wanted to observe, so I allowed it.

I started by processing the stones themselves. Some gems were beautiful left as they were, but cutting was necessary to bring out the unique brilliance of diamonds.

In my previous world, diamonds, rubies, sapphires, and emeralds were considered the four precious jewels. Diamonds were worth very much here, however. Furthermore, when it came to alexandrite, sapphire, and emerald, only the AAA grades were judged to have value. The remaining majority were worth very little.

"I guess I'll start with the sapphire," I announced.

"That gem isn't AAA. Are you sure it'll work?" asked Dia.

I wasn't surprised Dia noticed that. She was from a major noble family, and she had a keen eye when it came to gemstones. She was able to discern immediately that this gem was only AA grade.

"Yeah, it'll work. It'll be AAA before long," I answered.

What made a sapphire AAA was the depth of its coloration and the lack of impurities in the interior. Most unprocessed sapphires had a blue that was too faint, and they sported visible imperfections as well. However, 3 percent of sapphires possessed a deep hue and lacked many visible flaws.

The stone Maha procured for me had a faint color and lacked elegance, and, while not many, it did have some impurities. It was about as close to a AAA sapphire as a AA-graded stone could be. I was impressed that Maha obtained it on such short notice.

However, wearing it as it was in aristocratic society would get one ridiculed as a powerless noble presenting a sham in the hope of looking better than they really were.

Fortunately, a AA jewel could be made into a AAA with proper treatment.

"Precision Blaze."

This was a fire spell I'd modified to enable pinpoint accuracy. I was using that flame to perform a heat treatment on the sapphire. Heating one to 1,600 degrees Celsius triggered a chemical reaction that caused the stone's color to darken and eliminated interior flaws.

I worked with meticulous care. The heating wouldn't accomplish anything if the temperature was too low, and overexposure to the flame would ruin the sapphire. Maintaining such a precise temperature was mentally exhausting, even for me. My task here also went beyond just darkening the blue; I was aiming for a specific shade that would bring out Maha's intelligent charm.

After a little cheating with earth magic for a finishing touch, I was done.

"How does it look, Dia? Does it look AAA?" I asked.

"Yeah, that elegant blue is unmistakably the highest quality. That was amazing, Lugh. It's like magic," Dia praised.

"Well, I *was* using a spell... This result can be achieved without one, though." To pull it off without magic, you'd need large, specialized equipment and a great deal of expertise.

"It's also a spectacular shimmering hue. This is the first time I've ever seen the blue gleam so clearly," Dia added.

I nodded. "Well spotted. Yes, this sapphire sparkles blue."

That's one more thing I was intent on achieving. The beauty of sapphires didn't come from their color alone. Some contained silk inclusions that caused the blue to sparkle with glittering threads. The AAA status of a sapphire was decided not just by the depth of its shade but also by how it shimmered.

Heating sapphires normally made the silk inclusion disappear. The silk inclusions were nothing more than thin, rutile needles, and they melted under flame. That was why, even on Earth, sapphires with a deep shade of blue and no impurities without the need for heating were called "true sapphires" and sold for substantially higher prices.

Not even science could produce the shimmering blue. As such, true sapphires with rutile were extremely rare, and they were almost never put on the market. I, however, could cheat by using magic and just add the rutile after the heating treatment. That was impossible with technology alone.

"That blue gemstone is so beautiful. It's called a sapphire?" asked Tarte.

"Yeah, that's right. But that's no ordinary one. I've never seen a specimen this amazing before. Not even a princess would have one this impressive," Dia answered.

"It looks perfect because I treated it to look exactly the way I wanted it to, setting it apart from natural examples of its kind," I explained.

The difference between natural and processed gems was the ability to shape the latter into an ideal form. The faint blue of the jewel could be deepened to my ideal shade, and I was even able to add the silk inclusion. With the proper capabilities of a crafter, treated gemstones could surpass natural ones. This was, without a doubt, the most beautiful sapphire in this world.

"Okay, Maha's is done. I'll do the diamond next. This one will be a little dangerous, so keep your distance," I warned.

I chanted a new spell. About ten centimeters of water shot from my fingertips and hung in midair. The water then started to rotate at a very high speed while carrying a fine powder.

Dia's eyes were wide with interest. "Can you explain this spell?"

"I've named it Aqua Blade. It creates a high-pressure water current, then adds diamond powder and rotates it. Let's see... Throw one of those failed guns in the corner toward me," I instructed.

"Uh, okay," Dia responded, and she threw a firearm at me.

That gun was made out of an iron alloy, yet I sliced through it in midair. It was surreal seeing iron cut like butter without any resistance.

"As you can see, it's incredibly sharp," I said.

"That's insane," Dia replied.

"Diamond can't be cut with anything less. Unless you can find a harder metal, only diamond can be used to carve diamond."

Using Aqua Blade only made sense. It was time to get to work.

The diamond in front of me was of exceptional quality, even if this gemstone was considered second-rate by this world's standards. I sliced at it repeatedly using Aqua Blade, which could successfully cleave through even the hardest mineral in the world.

"Lord Lugh is so skilled," I heard Tarte say to Dia.

"I can't even see his hands. He must've carved the gem dozens of times already," Dia responded.

I ran my blade across the diamond over and over while in deep concentration. Then, at last, my work was done.

The diamond cut I chose was the most famous and traditional in existence—round brilliant. It was the image anyone pictured when they thought of diamonds. The form was the culmination of centuries of effort to achieve the greatest beauty a diamond could offer. I truly believed there was no surpassing this. After hundreds of years, a more beautiful cut still hadn't been discovered.

Bringing the round brilliant cut into this world kind of felt like cheating, but I saw no reason to hesitate when it was for Dia.

"It's done," I announced.

"*That's* a diamond?! I don't believe it!" Dia exclaimed.

Tarte marveled at my work. "It's captivating."

They were both taken by the beauty of the gemstone.

"This is the true beauty of diamonds. Ordinarily, they lack brilliance, but this is what you can achieve with the proper cut."

Diamonds have ruled as the kings of all gemstones since the technique to cut them was discovered, and that reputation was well-earned. People of this world would undoubtedly be mesmerized by the beauty of my labor.

The value and beauty of a gemstone weren't decided by appearance alone; rarity affected how they were seen as well. Diamonds weren't valued in this world. Even then, the diamond I just processed had the beauty to make anyone instantly rethink their opinion on the gemstone.

"...I'm exhausted. Heating the sapphire and cutting the diamond took a lot of mental energy. I'm going to take a break before I work on the emerald," I said. Improving the jewels had proved extremely demanding. The smallest mistake would have ruined the stones.

"It's only a thought, but wouldn't this diamond sell for a colossal price? It's certainly beautiful enough. Procuring diamonds can be done for cheap because of their low value, so you'd make a huge profit," Dia conjectured.

"I agree. This is the most beautiful gemstone I have ever

seen. I know that nobles and the wealthy would want it," added Tarte.

I gave a strained smile. "I'm sure. If we turned diamonds into a product, Natural You would rule the jewelry industry." I could already envision it. One who controlled diamonds would control the entire industry all over the world. That was how much power diamonds had.

Dia frowned. "It sounds like you don't want to do that. It'd be perfect for Natural You's customer base, though."

"From a business perspective, that's absolutely the right choice. But you're the only person I want to see wearing diamonds, Dia. A princess could ask me to make one, and I'd still refuse," I declared.

Dia would be the only person in this world to benefit from the brilliance of diamonds. Someone else would eventually obtain the technology to cut them, of course, but until then, they would shine only for Dia. That was the way I wanted it.

"You have a habit of saying the most pretentious things, Lugh."

"Do you not dislike that?"

"No, I love it."

Dia embraced me. That alone made all my effort today worthwhile.

All right, time to get back to work. I'm going to make the finest rings I can.

Last up was the emerald. Like diamonds and sapphires, emeralds were gemstones made more beautiful with treatment.

I began cutting it after performing an impregnation treatment. The process turned the stone's color to a jade hue, which effectively complemented Tarte's kind and gentle beauty.

It was now time for the final gem. I pulled out the alexandrite I'd obtained for Mom. Alexandrite was a captivating stone with two distinct faces: It shone bluish-green under daylight and a calming red under incandescent light from candles or lamps.

Most natural alexandrite was dull or didn't change color. Some jewels possessed vivid hues, but their color was unsatisfactory before or after the transformation. Alexandrite that changed color completely and was beautiful preceding and following the modification was extremely valuable and alluring. Finding it on the market wasn't easy, and it carried the value of a national treasure.

I knew how to treat alexandrite to make both the red and the green shades distinct and lovely. This was the only process that depended entirely on magic. It was a hopeless errand to rely on science alone. An incredibly enormous and precise machine would be required to do it right. Even with the level of technology in my previous world, it had never been realized outside of theory. Here, however, magic existed, allowing me to tamper with the stone's very composition.

I chose alexandrite because it was often associated with tranquility and passion. My mom constantly wore a gentle smile, yet carried a strong will within, so I thought this fit her perfectly.

It was hard work, but I got the result I wanted.

"I'm done treating the gemstones. Next, I'm gonna use them and the mithril to make the necklace and rings... Which means it's time for you two to leave," I said.

"What? I want to keep watching," Dia complained.

"I'm really interested to see how you make the jewelry," Tarte protested.

"If you see any more, it'll spoil your presents. I want you to be excited for the final products." I ushered them out of the room without listening to their arguments.

This was where the real work began. These ultimate gemstones were nothing more than materials. Whether I enhanced the beauty of the jewels or wasted them would come down to my designs.

Fortunately, I'd seen plenty of top-class accessories in this lifetime and my last. Using that knowledge as a model and relying on the sense I'd honed from years of observation, I would make each of the lovely women in my life an item more than suitable for them.

A full day had passed since I made the necklace and the rings. Dia and Tarte had been restless since morning. We were currently eating dinner, and I could feel them watching me. They were dying to see the rings I'd created for them.

Despite completing their gifts yesterday, I hadn't presented them yet, having chosen a specific day to do so.

I spoke up once we finished eating.

"I have a present for you, Mom. I haven't given you anything yet to celebrate your pregnancy," I said, and brought out the necklace. The alexandrite on the necklace sparkled. Its bluish-green color changed to red when exposed to candlelight.

My father's eyebrows twitched. He knew how much this was worth.

"Wow, what a beautiful necklace! ...It looks really expensive, though. I appreciate the thought, but I feel guilty about you spending so much money on me," my mother said.

"It wasn't that pricey," I responded.

"You're lying. Even I can see that. Cian, how much would this necklace sell for?" Mom asked Dad, believing that I was lying.

"Hmm... The metalwork is delicate and tasteful and was done using beautiful mithril. The alexandrite is of such high quality that not even AAA grade does it justice. It's five carats as well. Do you remember Count Lingrandt's mansion from the party we were invited to recently?" Cian asked.

"Yes. It was luxurious, beautiful, and so big."

"This necklace would easily buy that mansion. Attaching a price to it at all is nonsensical. This isn't an item that money can buy."

My mother's eyes widened in amazement. She obviously hadn't expected it to be worth quite that much. "I can't accept this! Please return it right away. You should use that money for yourself, Lugh!"

I'd expected her to say that, and I had a response ready. "It's okay, Mom. I made it myself, so it wasn't as expensive as it looks. The gemstone was only a AA grade. I treated it to enhance its beauty, and I did the metalwork myself," I explained. Alexandrite was relatively costly even when it wasn't AAA grade, but it wasn't too bad, considering my income.

"Are you telling the truth?" my mom pressed.

"Yes, I am. So please accept it. I worked very hard on it for you. I'd be sad to see you reject it," I insisted.

"Oh, that's not fair. How could I not agree after hearing that?" She was smiling despite her words. "Thank you. I'll cherish it," she said, and put the necklace on.

It looked great on her. No one would ridicule her behind her back in high society ever again. My mom didn't care about how others spoke of her, but I loved her, and I didn't want anyone bad-mouthing her. I wasn't going to say that out loud, for fear of being called a mama's boy, though.

I heard Dia's voice in my ear. She was using mana to send her words directly to me to keep anyone else from hearing.

"Wasn't the alexandrite bigger than that?"

She was right. My budget allowed me to purchase a sizable stone, and it was even larger when I completed treating it.

"It was too big for a necklace, so I cut it down. A bulky gem would lack class. This size suits Mom best."

"You're right, but I can't believe you actually did it... I would've felt like I wasted money."

The prevalent belief among the nobility was that the bigger the gemstone, the better. As such, price increased exponentially with size. The notion of cutting a jewel down to make it smaller was preposterous.

That trend was slowly changing, however. Progressive minds were tossing out the belief that bigger was always superior and were beginning to consider design and overall balance.

Furthermore, my mother was the kind of person to trust her sense of beauty over popular opinion. That's why I'd decided to make what I believed would be well-suited to her.

"How does it look on me?" my mother asked, blushing.

"It suits you just as well as I thought it would," I answered.

"Heh-heh, I'm so happy. What do you think, Cian?"

"It's beautiful... But I can't help but feel a little jealous." My dad answered with a rare bitter expression. He saw the confusion on Mom's face and continued. "There are two reasons for that. First, I'm jealous because you just accepted a necklace when I've tried so hard to get you to wear any gems other than your wedding ring."

"Oh, Cian. I'm so sorry. There was no way I could refuse a necklace that my little Lugh made for me. That doesn't mean I don't love you. What's the second reason?"

"Lugh gives you presents from time to time, but he's never offered me anything... It makes me a little sad."

Now that I thought about it... I got presents for my mother whenever she expressed a desire for something. I'd recently procured chocolate because she wanted some, and not long before that, I'd gone hunting for deer because she desired venison. Dad never asked for anything, though; I couldn't recall ever giving him a present.

"Sorry about that, Dad. Would you like these?" I inquired, retrieving some knives from my interior pockets.

I put three types of blades on the table. The first was a dagger I could throw at a moment's notice—I always carried a few of them with me. The second was an assassin's knife I concealed in my shoes or hem for a surprise attack. Last was an ordinary knife that I used as my primary weapon.

The daggers had a simple design because I hadn't refined them at all after producing them with magic, and I prioritized conceal-ability over functionality with the assassin's knife. Conversely, I'd processed the normal knife to further improve its capabilities after creating it with magic. My spells could only produce objects with simple shapes, so the framework of each weapon started out as very basic. If I sought to make something of real quality, I had to produce multiple pieces with magic and combine them. The normal knife was my main weapon, so I was particular about its design.

My dad undoubtedly appreciated the gifts. He smiled faintly and took the knives. I'd thought only of functionality when I made them, so they possessed no decoration whatsoever and appeared boorish for use by a noble. Even then, I trusted my father would understand their value.

"These knives are splendid. Thank you, Lugh. Sorry for mak-ing you feel like you had to give me something," he said.

"Don't worry about it. I've wanted to repay you for all you've done for me," I responded.

That was the truth. I was who I was today because of my dad's teachings. Being born into the Tuatha Dé household, spe-cifically to my parents, was the best thing that had ever happened to me.

"Then I'll gladly accept them. I'll prepare a gift for you in return." The way my dad said that made me think he'd been keeping his present for a while but hadn't known when to give it to me. This was a perfect excuse to do so.

"Hee-hee. We have the best son in the world. We're so blessed," my mother sang.

My father nodded. "That we are. Lugh has grown into a fine young man."

They smiled and poured alcohol for a toast. This was a little embarrassing.

"As happy as this made me, Lugh, there's one thing I need to warn you about. If you're going to give presents, you should prioritize Dia and Tarte over me. Girls are quick to get jealous, even at their man's mother," my mom cautioned, pointing a finger at me.

It was scary that gestures like that still suited a woman of her age.

"There's no need to worry about that. I have something in mind. I've prepared engagement rings for Dia, Tarte, and Maha, who I've told you about before," I explained.

"Truly? Well, goodness, what are you waiting for? You need to give them to the girls right away."

"I know, Mom. I'm getting engaged to all three of them, however, so I want to present the rings simultaneously. That's why I'm waiting. Maha can come over next week. I'm planning on throwing a party here. I want everyone to know that Lugh Tuatha Dé is betrothed."

There was special meaning in a noble's engagement. I'd made my intentions clear to Dia, Tarte, and Maha already. For commoners, that would've been sufficient, but as an aristocrat, I had a duty to spread the news of the development. If I didn't, my engagements would have no meaning.

Also, there would be no going back once the information was

out there. I would be a laughingstock if I canceled my pledges to marry.

"I give my approval. Cian...?" My mother looked to my father.

As head of House Tuatha Dé, my dad's decisions were absolute. If he was opposed to my intentions, I'd have no choice but to elope.

Had I been born to an ordinary noble family, I would not have been able to marry Dia, Tarte, and Maha. There was minimal political merit to our betrothals, after all. Truthfully, there was even less justification in my case, given the prestigious medical achievements of House Tuatha Dé, my Holy Knight status, and my multiple victories over demons. I could form a connection with any high-ranking noble family I wished.

"Very well. I will prepare for word to be sent out. If this is what you have set your heart upon, I will not oppose you, Son," my father said.

"Thank you, Dad."

"Do you have a time in mind for the marriage?"

"I'm thinking about delaying it until about a year after I graduate from the academy."

I'd resolved to save the world by then. My wedding would be held once that was done.

"That sounds fine to me... Children really do become adults in the blink of an eye. To think little Lugh is already speaking of marriage. Notify me once you know what day Maha is arriving. Let's give this top priority over all other business."

"Understood."

That took care of my family matters for the time being.

Now that I think about it, Dia and Tarte have been unusually silent. This matter concerned them directly, so I thought they'd have some input at the very least...

"Ooooh, this is all too sudden, Lugh," Dia said.

"I—I—I—I don't know what to do," Tarte stammered.

They had both frozen in place, faces scarlet. Perhaps I should've discussed this with them more beforehand.

Anyway, the engagement party was on. It would be best for me to invite all the nobles we were acquainted with and throw a grand affair, but my mother, father, and future wives wouldn't care for that. Thus, I intended to keep things within the family and make the event more intimate. The celebration was the perfect time to present the girls with their rings.

A few days had passed since I announced my engagement and sent messages throughout the country.

A carriage arrived at the Tuatha Dé estate, and I collected the packages and letters it delivered, inspecting them on the spot. The contents were almost entirely food. I planned to host a grand celebration for the engagement party tomorrow, and I'd procured quality ingredients without much concern for the expense.

The most eye-grabbing item was the giant lobster. Lobster spoiled very quickly and was rarely seen in inland domains like Tuatha Dé. I'd hired a mage to obtain freshly caught living lobster, freeze it in seawater, stuff it into a wooden box with sawdust, and cool the container at regular intervals during transport. By employing this method, we'd be able to enjoy lobster that tasted fresh, so long as I thawed it properly.

Hiring the mage for multiple days wasn't cheap, but lobster was one of Dia's favorite foods, justifying the effort and cost.

All these ingredients are of the highest quality.

I took this opportunity to retrieve a letter I intended to mail to Count Frantrude.

Count Frantrude was the man who'd been going to deliver false testimony against me to support a noble plotting to ruin me with fake accusations. By disguising myself as a woman named

Lulu, I'd won Count Frantrude's cooperation during the trial. Essentially, I seduced him to get what I wanted. It was a relatively common trick among assassins.

The easiest way to deal with the count would've been to kill him once his usefulness ended. However, I'd decided not to murder needlessly in this life. He'd done me a great service, after all, so I elected to settle things peacefully. I was putting a lot of time and effort into ending this without a fuss.

The plan was to have Count Frantrude grow distant with Lulu by planting numerous disagreements in her letters to him so that his love would fade gradually, bringing the relationship to a natural end. Instilling the count with the idea that things wouldn't work out, rather than giving him an outright rejection, made it far more likely that he'd get over me.

Despite that... I eyed at the letter with great disappointment. I'd exchanged many letters with Count Frantrude, but his passion for me had not subsided. He interpreted my words in ways that suited him, no matter what I wrote, and his feelings for Lulu grew stronger by the day.

I'd clearly underestimated him. Count Frantrude was an especially romantic person... No, that was wrong. He was merely a bigger idiot than I'd initially judged him to be. He only saw his ideal Lulu and remained ignorant of the disagreements I inserted into the letters. Lulu had become a perfect woman who existed only in his head.

"This is bad." I didn't want to dress up as a woman again, but I couldn't rule out the need. Worst case scenario, the count might travel uninvited to the home of the noblewoman whose name and identity I'd borrowed. That would expose my lie and lead to much greater trouble. Ending things directly in person was preferable to dealing with that kind of fiasco.

"Hmm? What's this?" One of the packages was addressed to Dia and Tarte. That was unusual. Maha had sent it.

The contents had to be quite large. From the weight, I thought they might be clothes. While wondering if I should open the parcel, I heard footsteps behind me and turned around.

Tarte, who'd been training under my father today, raced toward me. After snatching the package away and hugging it to her chest, she asked, "...Did you look inside?"

"No, I didn't," I answered.

"Thank goodness. That was close."

Tarte was still in her training clothes. She must have sprinted here upon realizing that the carriage had arrived. I was interested to know the contents of the delivery, but I didn't ask. If Tarte was willing to tell me, she wouldn't have rushed here like that.

That my father let Tarte out of training was surprising. He was typically a very strict teacher.

"How was practice with Dad?" I inquired, changing the topic to hide my curiosity.

"I learned a lot. His assassination methods resemble yours, but they're slightly different. It was interesting. He even taught me some new tricks!"

I normally oversaw Tarte's instruction, but today's session was special. My dad was conducting House Tuatha Dé's version of marriage training. I remembered Mom complaining about it in the past. She'd received this baptism into the family immediately after her wedding, and she'd grumbled that it was so hard it made her want to die.

An assassin's family could be their greatest weakness. To account for that, all members of the Tuatha Dé clan were taught the bare minimum of self-defense techniques. That "bare minimum" was very difficult to achieve, though.

"Really? You'll have to teach me some of those tricks later," I said.

"Sure thing, my lord! Are all those packages in the back of the carriage ingredients for the party? Wow, that's amazing! That lobster's huge! I never imagined we would eat seafood in Tuatha Dé!"

"I'm planning on making a lot of fun dishes for the party."

"I'm not allowed to help, am I?"

"I'll be doing it all myself. I want to surprise everyone."

I was having a little fun with the cooking this time, going for something I'd intentionally never done before.

"I can't wait to see the result."

"Didn't expect you to give up so easily."

"Well, *we* have our own sur— *Ahem, ahem.* Uh, well, I need to return to my training. I'll see you later!" Tarte dashed off as swiftly as she'd arrived, with her parcel in her arms. No matter how much time passed, that clumsy part of her would never change.

I returned to my room with some letters that had arrived with the other deliveries. There were four of them, all addressed to me.

The first was Maha's report regarding Natural You. She concisely summed up last month's financial situation and the progress of our business plans.

Given the increase in monster numbers, the stagnation of trade, and the worsening economy, many enterprises were in the red. Bucking the trend, Natural You had shown firm growth over the past year.

The catch was that cosmetics sales were experiencing negative growth for the first time since the founding of Natural You. It was inevitable that beauty products would be the first to go during hard times. Our cosmetics department was still in the black, but there was no way to put a positive spin on the number.

We made up for the decline in makeup sales with a new product aimed at the military. According to Maha's report, the item was very well received on the field, and we were likely to strike a long-term deal to supply it in large quantities. That would give Natural You stability.

The prospects for success were good... But I didn't expect it to be this *popular.*

The product Natural You produced for the army was an energy drink. Put simply, it was a beverage pumped full of sugar, caffeine, and vitamins. These were the main ingredients of energy drinks in my previous world as well, and any other additives could be easily substituted or omitted. The effect of the beverage was considerable and, while temporary, made exhaustion vanish in an instant. There was no precedent for such a beverage here, and the response to it was tremendous.

The second letter is from the Royal Knights Academy.

The message explained that repairs were complete and that the academy would reopen the week after next. That was good news, but one thing in the missive irritated me. The academy staff wished to hold a ceremony to commemorate my extermination of the earth dragon demon.

I understood their motive. The school had been destroyed by a demon, giving many the impression that it was unsafe. They needed to clear away that image. To that end, they were going to hold a lavish celebration to let students and their families know they would be safe because of my presence.

"I guess I can put up with it. I don't have any dislike for the academy itself." It would also be nice to see Dia and Tarte in uniform again.

Now, for the third letter...

"It's from Nevan. That was faster than I expected."

This message had come from Nevan Romalung, daughter of one of the four major dukedoms. As it happened, she was very interested in marrying me.

The other day, I asked Dad to spread the word of my future marriages to Dia, Tarte, and Maha. When a noble got engaged, a written form had to be submitted to the administrator of their region declaring their intention. The administrator then conveyed that information to their subservient nobles below them and to the central government, after which the news spread through aristocratic society. It was a noble's duty to report their betrothal. Failing to do so meant the engagement couldn't become official.

The administrator of this region was Margrave Ailrush, and the Romalung dukedom was stationed above him. It had only been a matter of time before Nevan found out.

It seemed like she didn't intend to obstruct my engagements. Rather, she expressed her relief to learn that I was in favor of marriage and that I was indeed attracted to women. She also offered her congratulations. I was concerned about the bit where she asserted that four wives would be just as easy as three, but I didn't need to worry about that for the moment.

On to the fourth letter.

"I don't want to deal with this, but I knew it was going to happen."

The final missive was from Margrave Ailrush. To summarize, the letter instructed me to hold an engagement party for all nobles of this region, including the margrave himself and the big shot aristocrats from the royal capital. He called the message a warning, but it read more like a command. Margrave Ailrush had also sent a letter to Dad, likely demanding the same thing.

By rules alone, all we had to do was report to the region administrator for the betrothal to be made official. Despite that, it was common practice among nobles to throw a party and invite other aristocrats with whom they were on cordial terms when an heir got engaged.

I wrote a reply. It was a plain refusal. I was aware of what I should've done in my position, but I wanted no part of a celebration with a bunch of nobles I wasn't particularly close with. It would be exhausting, and watching the ignorant fools appraise Dia, Tarte, and Maha with their vulgar gazes would be insufferable.

I also recognized Margrave Ailrush's ulterior motive. If the Holy Knight threw an engagement party, all of the most influential nobles in the capital would attend. This was the best chance the margrave would ever have to form connections in the capital. Undoubtedly, he was dying for a chance to complain about me rising above my station as a lowly Tuatha Dé, too.

No way in hell was I going to put up with that. I would leave the struggle for rank and power in high society to the aristocrats who lived for it.

I finished my letter and instructed a servant to send it.

"That takes care of that. I suppose I should get started on preparations for the cooking."

I needed to pick up Maha tomorrow, so today had to be spent getting as much of the food ready as possible.

The next day, I used an aircraft to pick up Maha and bring her to Tuatha Dé. Maha fell to her knees, pale-faced, when I landed and helped her down. She put her hands over her mouth to keep from vomiting. Tarte and Dia had adapted to their first flight without any difficulty, but that was unusual; this was how most people would end up feeling.

"Are you okay?" I asked.

"...That was really difficult, but yes. You've told me about aircraft before, but they're even more capable than I imagined. This would cause a revolution in the world of distribution if it was mass-produced. Taking days by carriage to get to a business meeting seems absurd to me now," Maha answered.

"Mass production would be difficult. Riding on the wind alone isn't so hard, but flying between cities like we just did requires significant mana capacity and control."

"I realize that, but I still want it. Making the telecommunications network public would be even better, but that isn't an option..."

If we made the telecommunications network available to the general public, there would be no need to travel to other towns at all. That was highly classified information, however. The value of instant long-distance communication was immeasurable in this world, and more countries than could be counted on two hands would start a war to obtain that technology.

The lack of long-distance communication was why merchants needed to purchase an expensive escort to protect them on long, sluggish journeys by carriage that could take days or even a month.

"I understand why you want an aircraft. If you had one, you'd be able to make trips in hours that used to take you days. That would give you room in your schedule," I said.

"Yes, exactly. Travel time is such a waste and greatly limits what I can do in business," Maha responded.

Time was more precious than anything to a busy manager. That was especially true for Maha, who bustled all about the country year-round for work.

The problem was that Maha's mana capacity was lower than average. Her mana control was superior to Tarte's, and she was one of the most talented people I knew, but... This request was very like her.

"I'll think about it. I could make a chargeable version with Fahr Stones attached. If I engraved a formula into the aircraft to automatically cast a spell that calls wind, you would be able to pilot it. I'll make one as a test."

I'd worked out the technique of engraving formulas into material by analyzing a divine treasure, but this one would require minute control. It was going to be quite difficult to make. However, I'd gladly put in the effort for Maha. It was nothing compared to the work she had put in for me.

"I'm happy to hear it. I can't wait!" Maha beamed. That smile alone would make all the effort worth it.

With all the cooking finished, I carried the food to the party venue before the festivities began. Although we barely used it, we did have a room for this purpose. I told everyone that not a single person could enter until the designated time. Maha went to Tarte's room to wait for the start of the celebration after she arrived.

"Phew, I managed to finish everything in time." I surveyed the room, satisfied with my work. The decorations were to my liking, and I had arranged the cuisine as a buffet.

I placed the entrées on large plates and used hot water to heat the dishes and prevent any warm foods from going cold, a method employed at hotels. Because flame wasn't applied to anything directly, nothing was burned or boiled down. The heat was coming from Fahr Stones submerged in the water. I was keeping cold food chilled with ice.

Half of the meal I'd prepared was home cooking that represented the tastes of our domain. This included cream stew, pheasant roast, Dia's favorite gratin, salt-grilled runamass, salad with vegetables picked in Tuatha Dé, soybean bread, and more.

The other half of the menu consisted of luxurious and unusual dishes. One example was *unagi kabayaki*, or grilled eel. There were no eels in Tuatha Dé, but they were quite popular in towns to the south.

I'd obtained live eels, then used fish sauce in place of soy sauce, instilled sweetness with honey and wine, lathered them with sauce with added richness from butter, and grilled them over charcoal. It was essentially Western-style *kabayaki*, which I knew would fit my family's tastes better. Stewing eel was a common practice in this world, so grilled eel was going to surprise them.

For the meat, I'd obtained popular beef from cows raised in the capital only for eating, and I'd created two separate dishes. The first was splendid roast beef prepared using low-temperature cooking. The second was a pulpy beef stew made using gelatin-rich cheek and tail meat stewed in special demi-glacé. I was proud of both.

The lobster that I took great pains to have delivered filled the seafood role. Just like the meat, there were two seafood dishes. The first was lobster carpaccio, and the second was fried lobster that I cooked rare to bring out the sweetness as much as possible.

Desert was my favorite cake, one hailed as the greatest chocolate cake ever devised.

I'd cooked all these dishes using my knowledge from my previous life, and none of them had ever been tasted in this world. My parents and I rarely indulged ourselves like this. That didn't mean I disliked doing so, however. It was good to cut loose at times like this, and there were familiar foods to choose from in case anyone grew tired of the luxurious options.

I'd always believed food to be one of the most critical elements of a party. Eating a good meal was enough to lift the spirits of the attendees, which in turn made everything else more enjoyable. That was why I went all out with the cooking.

"It's about time." I looked at my watch and saw that the festivities would begin at any moment.

Mom and Dad arrived first. They were wearing their finest clothes, and Mom had the alexandrite necklace I gave her around her neck. It looked great on her. I complimented her, and she gave an embarrassed reaction.

My three fiancées entered next.

"You all look beautiful," I said, bewitched by their appearances. They were all wearing dresses I'd never seen before.

These dresses must be what Maha sent to Dia and Tarte. It explained why Tarte was so desperate to hide them from me.

"Hee-hee, you're always surprising us, Lugh, so this time, we thought we'd get back at you a little," said Dia.

"Um, does this look good on me?" Tarte asked shyly.

"You're so blessed, dear brother, getting engaged to three lovely young women," Maha remarked.

I smiled. Maha was right. Each of them was enchanting. Maha must have chosen the outfits; each one suited its wearer exquisitely. I couldn't wait to see the girls wearing my engagement rings.

"...You got me. Now, if you three would move to the center of the room. Let's get this party underway. It's time to celebrate our engagements."

Three beautiful fiancées, my loving parents, and an extravagant feast. This would be a truly great day.

I opened a bottle of wine. It was time to start the party.

I'd elected to make the celebration a standing buffet, placing a trio of small bar tables in the middle of the room and the food along the walls. This setup allowed everyone to grab the food they wanted and speak with whoever they pleased while eating.

"Start by filling your plates. We'll toast after that," I announced.

"Wow, there's so much food I don't even know where to start. Ah, gratin! You put it in the shell of a crab. That's so cute. Thank you for making my favorite food, Lugh!" Dia said excitedly.

Gratin always looked sloppy and gross after being picked at. I didn't want that to happen, so I poured it into small crab shells and baked them together. To keep the rest of the crab from going to waste, I cooked the meat into the gratin and used crab butter for the sauce, creating a high-quality crab gratin. The appearance and the taste complemented each other well.

"Everything looks so delicious that it's hard to choose," Tarte expressed.

"It's been a long time since I've eaten your cooking, dear brother. I could think of no better feast than one prepared by you," Maha stated.

"This looks incredible, Cian," my mother said.

Grinning, my father answered, "That it does. Let's grab some food."

I chose this format for the party even though there were only six attendees because my parents said they wanted time to speak with each of my fiancées individually. If this had been a seated party, we would've had to change seats frequently, which was an unpleasant notion. Dia had also mentioned that she hoped to talk to Maha alone, and Tarte and Maha were great friends and likely had a lot built up to talk about.

They truly are beautiful. I observed my fiancées again. The dresses Maha had selected looked stunning on them.

Dia's dress was primarily white and had many frills. She resembled a lovely fairy. Tarte was draped in a puffy yellow dress that showed a bold amount of cleavage. The red accents on the outfit suited her warm personality. It was also sexy. Maha wore a mature purple dress that she pulled off flawlessly. Slits revealed her legs. She was beautiful, stylish, and alluring.

Each garment had been crafted by an elite designer with the very best materials. That Maha procured them on such short notice was truly impressive.

"Looks like everyone's gotten some food. I'd like to give a short speech before the toast. First, I want to thank Dia, Tarte, and Maha for falling in love with me. All three of you are beautiful and talented. You each could've chosen any man, and I am happy you all picked me. That selection wasn't a mistake, and I'll prove that to you every day of our lives moving forward."

I've always hated humility. It was common at times like this to be self-deprecating as you thanked your fiancée for choosing you. "I don't know what she sees in me," "I don't deserve her," and the like. However, that would be like telling the girls that they lacked a discerning eye for men. I wouldn't insult them like that.

That was why I declared that choosing me was not a mistake. I realized that I was only making things harder on myself by saying that, but if I couldn't follow through on that promise, I didn't deserve them.

"I will make all of you happy. I do have one request, though. Please do your best to bring me joy as well. If we all work together to bring bliss to each other's lives, we'll build a greater future than I could achieve through my efforts alone. Mom and Dad are the perfect examples. I want to make a household as warm as the one they have."

Before my reincarnation, I'd existed only as a tool for killing. I knew nothing of the preciousness and warmth of life.

I'd considered familial and romantic love as nothing more than methods to help my assassinations. I'd bedded too many people to count and whispered sweet nothings into their ears, but my words were always hollow. It was only after I was born into the Tuatha Dé family under my loving parents that love became real to me.

My parents changed me from a tool into a person. I was grateful for that, and I admired them deeply.

"Of course, Lugh. I don't want this to be a one-sided relationship," Dia responded.

"I am yours, Lord Lugh. Our engagement does nothing to change the fact that I live for you!" Tarte declared.

"I feel the same way as Tarte. I am going to loosen my self-restraint a little, though," Maha replied.

That was what I wanted to hear. I was deeply touched. That

I could feel such excitement without a hint of unease proved that they were the perfect partners for me.

"That's all from me. Let's move to the toast," I said.

We all raised our glasses. The alcohol I poured was a local one made in Tuatha Dé. The main ingredient was maple syrup. Maple syrup could only be harvested during a very small period of time in winter, and a single tree didn't produce that much of it. It was used up before it ever made it out of our domain, making it a luxury only citizens of Tuatha Dé got to enjoy. That was why I chose this alcohol for the toast of our engagement party.

"Cheers!"

We clinked our glasses together and smiled. With that, the true festivities began.

My parents got right to work on their interviews with my fiancées, summoning Maha first. Given this, Dia, Tarte, and I sat at one table, while my mother and father took another with Maha.

Grinning, Dia said, "Heh-heh, I think I'll start with the gratin you made for me."

"Some things never change," I said.

"I, for one, think it's weird how you always save the best for last, Lugh. Food tastes the best if you eat it while you're hungry. Wow, this crab gratin is incredible!"

We clearly had different preferences when it came to dining. I've always liked to save my favorite part of the meal for last.

"Um, what is this fluffy fish?! This is the most delicious fish I have ever tasted!" gushed Tarte.

"That's eel. This is the best way to eat it."

The food was well received, and enthusiasm swelled in the room. Dia and Tarte were eating much more than usual. I glanced at Maha and saw her enjoying a lively conversation with my parents, despite their having never met before. Her social skills were unrivaled. Mingling in high society and enduring its rampant wickedness on a daily basis as the proxy representative of Natural You was something not many could pull off.

"Maha is so pretty," Dia commented.

"I'm jealous. She's so mature. I can't believe she's the same age as me," Tarte lamented.

Maha's appearance, manner, and way of speech were all elegant. Much of that was natural, but she wouldn't have achieved this level of refinement without hard work as well. People became recognized as adults at fourteen in this country, and while most retained some childish behavior at that age, there was no sign of that with Maha. It gave her an edge.

"While you two aren't on her level, you can both act mature enough on formal occasions. You do have a habit of letting your true personalities emerge at times, however... What sets Maha apart is her ability to keep it up all the time."

Dia and Tarte were very attractive, and more than looked the part for high society. They were both perfectly capable of utilizing that; Dia had received thorough drilling in the art of etiquette as the daughter of Count Viekone, and I'd trained Tarte to serve flawlessly as the maid of a noble without embarrassing herself or me. Even then, they couldn't maintain it at every moment.

"I just lose all desire to put on the act if I'm not in that kind of situation," Dia admitted.

Tarte nodded. "Me too. I think being able to keep it going twenty-four seven as Maha does is a talent."

I wasn't about to disagree. That said, Maha behaved like an ordinary teenage girl when we were alone together, but I kept that a secret.

Maha returned to our table, and Dia stood to join my parents.

"Welcome back. What did Mom and Dad say?" I asked.

"They asked me to take care of you," Maha answered.

"You were able to gain their approval, then?"

"They approved of me from the start. They said that they trusted your judgment in women absolutely. They only wanted peace of mind. I told them what kind of person I was without holding anything back."

My parents really had faith in me.

"That's good to hear."

"Yeah. I'm relieved that they seem like good people. I think it went quite well. I do have one problem, however. I want to continue managing Natural You, but we can't exactly uproot the family from Tuatha Dé... Finding a way to live together is going to be difficult."

That was true. We couldn't abandon the Tuatha Dé domain, and Maha couldn't quit Natural You. The company did business all throughout the country, or rather, all throughout the world, but its center was still the flagship store in Milteu. As the largest port city in the country, Milteu was a hub for information and distribution. Moving from there was a lethal blow for a merchant.

"I'll go to see you as often as I can. How about I bring Mom and Dad next time so we can go sightseeing together?" I offered.

Maha sighed. "...I've been able to put up with it until now, but living apart after marriage would be miserable. So I have a proposal for you."

"I have a bad feeling about this."

"Let's move the flagship store of Natural You here."

"What do you think you'll be able to accomplish after migrating the flagship store to a rural region like this?"

"I'm going to develop Tuatha Dé into an even greater region than Milteu. If I can do that, then the store won't be out of place here at all."

I couldn't believe what Maha was saying. Milteu had become what it was largely because of its advantageous location. It was right in the middle of the nation, making it easy to travel to. The surrounding highways were well-maintained, and it was the country's largest port, making transport of goods very easy.

Tuatha Dé, on the other hand, was located on the western edge of Alvan. It possessed no access to the ocean. There wasn't even a river large enough for ships to pass through. Even traveling here by land was difficult because of the mountains in the way. It was an incredibly unfavorable headquarters region for distribution.

"Developing Tuatha Dé into a city of commerce is unrealistic," I stated.

"I'm aware of that, but I have a plan to make it possible. You're going to be impressed. It will likely take more than a decade to achieve, though," Maha replied.

"I suppose you intend to keep the details of this scheme a secret from me."

"Yes, it'll be more fun that way."

Well, knowing Maha, I doubt any bad will come of it. She wouldn't change Tuatha Dé in a way I disapproved of.

We continued to talk until Dia's conversation with my parents finished. Dia walked…to the food along the walls, not back to us. This time she picked out some fried lobster. Tarte went over to my parents after my mom beckoned to her. Dia returned to my table shortly after.

"Wow, this is tender and sweet. The sour sauce is amazing, too. Ahh, this is bliss," Dia said, very clearly delighted.

"...So? What do you think?" I questioned.

"It's absolutely delicious."

"I meant your talk with my parents."

"It was fine. They got all excited, pressing me to have children as quickly as possible, and made sure I knew that even though I'm the first wife, the heir may not end up being mine because the most talented child will be chosen. You know, typical stuff."

"Sounds fairly heavy to me." Only a trueborn noble like Dia would regard such discussion so lightly.

"It's only logical that the most talented child will inherit the house. Besides, I'm pretty confident it will be one of mine. The women of House Viekone always bear strong offspring. You're going to love our kids. I'll work hard as your wife!"

That wasn't some unfounded belief but the plain truth. After all, my mom—a Viekone woman—gave birth to me, the greatest Tuatha Dé in history, and Dia was once targeted by prominent nobles in Soigel who wanted to kidnap her.

I was born as Lugh Tuatha Dé because the goddess judged him to be the most gifted child among all of humanity. It was astounding that my mother gave birth to a child who surpassed any of House Romalung, which had performed centuries of selective breeding. The Viekone blood was what made that possible.

My mom was once targeted by nobles just like Dia was, and my dad was the one who took her to safety. I couldn't believe it when he told me that story. He'd displayed a passion and recklessness that I couldn't imagine from him now, and I didn't know that side of him ever existed.

"You don't have to worry about that. I just want my kids to be happy," I said. I wanted to treasure all my children, regardless of how talented they were.

"I'll love my kids no matter what, but they'll be safer the more capable they are. Nobles inevitably lead difficult lives. I'm going to raise them to be strong, for their own sakes. I'll be a strict teacher!" Dia declared.

"Don't be too hard on them."

"Hmm, I don't think you're one to talk, Lugh. You'd push them way harder than me. You turn into a demon during our training sessions."

"I don't think I'm severe, though."

All I did was analyze Dia's and Tarte's bodies and push them to maximum efficiency within their physical limits. I wasn't over-working them.

"Whatever you say, Lugh. Ah, Tarte's back."

Tarte returned to our table.

"Did it go all right?" I asked.

"Y-yes. They, um, gave me lots of advice about becoming the wife of a noble. They said I should be prepared for comments regarding my birth when attending functions in high society, and other stuff like that. I will keep what they said in mind," Tarte answered.

My parents focused on giving her advice rather than judging her for their approval. Tarte had lived with us for years now, and had basically been a member of our family. My mother and father probably had nothing left to test her on at this point.

"They also said that you are passive regarding women, so it

would be best for me to take the lead. Mom said that she would, um, teach me a really effective trick to...get you in the mood," Tarte continued, blushing deep red at that last part.

I couldn't believe that woman sometimes.

"...You don't need to think about that too much."

"Yes, my lord. I will do my best!"

I was extremely worried about that. I would need to be careful around Tarte for a while. I didn't dislike sexual advances from her, but I had my pride to think of.

My parents summoned me next. What did they want to discuss?

I walked over to my parents' table. They both wore serious expressions. I was used to that from my father, but it was an unusual sight from my mother.

"Your fiancées are all wonderful people. It appears you have great taste in women, in addition to all your other talents," my father said.

"You did great, Lugh! I'm so happy I'm gaining three wonderful daughters," my mother cheered, giving me a thumbs-up.

"Yeah, they're all great girls," I agreed.

"That said, taking all of them as your wives will be difficult. Esri alone has been more than enough of a handful for me," my father stated.

With a shallow smile, my mother asked, "Whatever do you mean by that?"

"*Ahem*... Suffice it to say, marriage is a difficult endeavor," my father cautioned.

"I am aware of that. I made this decision with the resolve to make all of them happy. No matter how hard our lives turn out to be, it will be better than seeing them snatched up by other men," I responded.

Marrying all three of them hadn't been my initial plan. I thought I would pick one eventually, and that I would support any of them if they chose another husband.

But when I watched someone propose to Maha while I was already bound romantically to Dia and Tarte, I was overcome by intense feelings of loss, fear, and anger at the thought of having her stolen from me. It was at that moment that I made up my mind. I wouldn't let any of them go. I would make all of them happy.

I was convinced that the joy we gained would make up for any difficulties we encountered. I also decided that if I was going to persist in this selfishness, I needed to give them better lives than any other man in the world could.

"It's good that you're going into this with the right mindset. Now you must follow through on your word." There was a stern look in my father's eyes.

"Naturally. I know I am capable of it. That's the kind of person you raised me to be, after all," I assured him.

"Goodness, my little Lugh has become such a fine young man. I want to see my grandchildren's faces as soon as possible, so I expect you to get right to work!" my mother said.

"You'll have to wait a little longer for that."

My plan was to not have children until after I saved the world. In addition to being my fiancées, Dia, Tarte, and Maha were essential in my battle against the demons.

"Meanie," Mom said, glaring at me. She wasn't going to bend on that desire.

We talked about the future next. Both my parents were smiling. At the next table, my three fiancées were having fun chatting without me. Given this warm family environment, I knew things were going to go well. They were all such good people.

I would give my all to protect this happiness. And as I mused upon that determination, the engagement party ran late into the night.

My celebration concluded without issue. My parents and fiancées had a great time.

At the end of the party, I handed the girls the engagement rings I'd made for them, and I treated everyone to Sacher torte, the most famous chocolate cake in my previous world. Everyone was utterly enchanted by the taste, and it wasn't surprising. The recipe was so good that it had once caused a legal battle. Maha went full merchant-mode when she tried the cake, which was funny to see.

It was truly a day to remember.

When dawn came the next day, it was time to take Maha back to Milteu. My mother took her hands to bid her farewell. "I wish you had taken more time to relax here, Maha."

"I would've liked to, but I have to get back to work. I can't neglect the company that Lugh entrusted to me." Maha responded with a slightly lonely expression.

"I'll visit you," I said.

"I'll be waiting. I feel like this ring has given me renewed energy." The sapphire shone blue on her finger.

"I'll go with you next time. I wanted to talk to you some more, Maha," Dia added.

Maha smiled. "I'm happy to hear that. I was just thinking the same thing, Dia."

The two girls had become good friends in the span of a single day. That Maha wasn't addressing Dia as "Lady Dia" was proof of that. They'd hit it off right away and had lots of fun talking to each other. Given their differing interests and personalities, I didn't expect them to get along so well.

Now that I thought about it, though, it shouldn't have been a surprise. Dia was a sorcerer, and Maha was a merchant; they followed different paths, but they were both professionals in their respective fields. They surely shared common ground.

"All right, we need to go," Maha announced.

"Be careful," called Tarte.

"Bring us back some souvenirs," Dia requested.

Once we said our good-byes, I took off with Maha in the aircraft.

A few days had come and gone since I flew Maha back to Milteu. Recent events were giving me a headache.

The reaction to the news of my engagements was larger than I expected. Nobles near the Tuatha Dé domain were sent into an absolute frenzy once I received a congratulatory gift directly from the royal family.

People had assumed I stood in high favor with the royal family because of my heroic deeds in killing demons, and this confirmed it. Now everyone was losing their minds trying to cozy up to House Tuatha Dé. My father and I laughed at the tenfold increase in the number of people claiming to be friends and relatives of our family. Nobles had great authority in the Alvanian Kingdom, but the royal family still reigned supreme.

Things got further out of hand when two of the four major dukedoms sent me a congratulatory present. That caused the already large number of marriage proposals I was receiving to snowball into a true avalanche. In my previous world, it would have been absurd to propose to someone who had just announced their engagement, but this country allowed polygamy. And since I had multiple fiancées already, many families were taking the chance to see if they could throw one of their daughters onto the altar as well. My fiancées not being from local aristocratic families spurred people on even more.

To sum up, everyone wanted to bring me into their family because I had the favor of the royal family and a couple of the four major dukedoms.

The higher-ranking nobles commanding me to take their daughters as my first wife, adding that they'll tolerate Dia, Tarte, and Maha if I do so, are really irritating me. House Tuatha Dé was a lowly barony, so there were times when we had to obey those above us. However, the insulting words toward my fiancées ensured that I wouldn't do so this time.

I just have to endure this for a few more days. We were returning to the academy next week. That would free me from these irritating duties, at least momentarily... I was sure some girls at school would approach me on instructions from their families, but noble rank was not supposed to matter at the academy. It was an official stance that not everyone abided by, but the policy had been instated by the royal family. That meant I'd be free to ignore my duties.

The communications device in my room rang. It was Maha's channel.

"Huh, you're in your room this time," she said.

"Yeah, I'm just mindlessly writing rejections to the avalanche of marriage proposals I've received."

"Sounds like you've had it rough, too."

"'Too?' So things are busy at Natural You?"

"Of course. The proxy representative of the company is one of the future wives of Lugh Tuatha Dé, the world's exciting young demon slayer."

"Oh yeah… I didn't think about that. Maybe I should have delayed my engagements a little longer."

"No way. I've been over the moon since you made your feelings for me clear, dear brother. Anyway, I called to give you my regular report. There's no sign of demon activity at the moment."

"I see. Thanks."

Lately, it seemed the surge in monster appearances had died down. That made me suspicious that the demons were plotting something and kept me on high alert. Yet as Maha said, there was no sign of demon activity.

I did, however, receive reports of worrying news from an entirely different party… It seemed that the church was up to no good.

"You're welcome. These reports are going to get difficult next week. Extending the telecommunications network to the academy will be very risky."

"I have a few ideas. I'll figure something out in the next few days."

Installing the cables and terminals of the telecommunications network at the academy would be a greater challenge than in an ordinary city. However, it wasn't impossible.

"That's a relief. I'd hate not being able to hear your voice anymore. I'm going to hang up. Until our next report."

"Keep up the good work."

She hung up. It sounded like Maha was having a rough time. I thought it might be a good idea to stop by the company as Illig Balor. I began considering the most effective time to make an appearance.

The academy's restoration was completed according to the schedule mentioned in the letter, and it reopened at last. Dia, Tarte, and I alighted from our carriage and walked through the gate. It had been a long time since I'd seen Dia and Tarte in their school uniforms.

Most of the students I saw seemed happy to be reunited with their friends.

"We're getting so much attention," Tarte commented.

"We've accomplished a lot since the academy closed. Or rather, Lugh has," Dia responded.

All eyes turned our way as we moved through the academy grounds. We'd become total celebrities.

One of the reasons we garnered so many gazes was the unrivaled beauty of Dia and Tarte paired with the engagement rings on their fingers. After receiving them, they'd hardly removed their rings except to bathe and sleep. I occasionally caught them spacing out and staring at their rings in silence. Seeing the two like that brought me great joy.

I was wearing a ring, too, naturally. It was a silver band without a gemstone. It wasn't ordinary silver, though. I'd imbued it with several unique capabilities.

"I'm not accustomed to having so many people watching me," I admitted.

"Well, you'd better get used to it. You're only going to attract more and more attention from now on," Dia advised.

"Surely not."

"You definitely will. I can't imagine you sitting back and fading into obscurity."

"Tarte, help me out here."

"...Ah-ha-ha, I actually agree with Lady Dia."

I couldn't believe even Tarte thought as much. I supposed I only had myself to blame for this.

The students observed me from a distance, none seemingly possessed of sufficient courage to approach. There was an exception, however, a student who'd agreed to avoid speaking with me before the incident that closed the academy. She was also quite famous and was head of the year above Dia, Tarte, and me. She'd been away on an expedition at the time of the orc demon attack. Had she been present, the damage likely would have been only half as bad. That was how remarkable a person she was.

"Lugh Tuatha Dé, I have something I wish to discuss with you. Would you accompany me to my apartment?" she requested.

It was Nevan Romalung, a daughter of House Romalung and a masterpiece resulting from centuries of work to create the ultimate humans.

"I would be glad to, Ms. Romalung," I answered, addressing her formally because of her status as an upperclassman.

Girls squealed all around us. I'd heard that Nevan was just as popular with them as she was with boys, but it was surprising to see firsthand.

The students were taking great interest in this pairing of two famous people. We hadn't interacted at the academy previously because Duke Romalung oversaw the Tuatha Dé assassination jobs and approved hit requests handed down from the royal family.

Initially, we couldn't afford to betray that connection between our two families. I was the son of a baron, and she was the daughter of a duke; our ranks differed too significantly, and being overly friendly might have aroused suspicion. The situation had since changed, however. I was accomplished enough that there was nothing strange about a duke's daughter approaching me.

The two of us walked together, and Nevan spoke to me using a special vocalization method so that only I could hear her.

"Your new fame makes our work much easier."

"My father filled me in. I understand you have a job so important you must give it to me directly instead of entrusting it to your intelligence agents. I have to admit, that makes me a tad concerned."

Before leaving for the academy, my father had informed me that there was a new assassination job. Normally, House Romalung had their intelligence agents deliver us an encrypted missive. Their agents were the best of the best, and their cipher was incredibly complex. On the very small chance a letter was intercepted, no one would ever be able to decode it.

Truthfully, not one of their jobs for us had ever leaked. For Nevan to explain the task in her quarters at the academy despite that meant the topic could only be discussed in the most secure location possible.

"This request will surprise you... It stands in defiance of the gods themselves."

I had a good idea of what this was going to be. Plenty of signs were hidden within the reports from my information network. If my guess was correct, just voicing hostility toward this target, let alone killing them, would be enough to get the perpetrator and their entire family executed. This could end up being the most difficult assassination I'd ever taken on, in this life or my last.

"What a thoughtful engagement present."

"I'm glad you like it... Also, just so you know, if I'd been one of your fiancées and a member of your family, I still would have given you this job."

Nevan had decided as a Romalung, without letting her feelings influence her decision, that this target needed to be killed for the country's wellbeing. That meant that, as a Tuatha Dé, it was my duty to face this challenge. I would hear Nevan out, and if I decided it was in the best interest of the Alvanian Kingdom, I would do my duty.

We went to the Class S dorm and walked to the top floor, where the upperclassmen lived. I instructed Dia and Tarte to go to our apartment.

There's too much about this situation I don't like.

If I decided this was a job I shouldn't accept, it would be better for Dia and Tarte if they were kept ignorant of the details. House Romalung was delivering this job directly, and if I refused, they might decide to remove anyone who knew too much.

I entered Nevan's apartment. Its layout was identical to mine, but the interior put her tastes and sophisticated sense of aesthetics on full display.

"This room suits you well, Nevan," I remarked.

"Is that a compliment?" she asked.

"Yes. It has all the elegance of a noble lady."

Her quarters were decorated with beautiful furnishings and bright, showy colors. It could easily have come off as coarse, but that wasn't the case. The room had a refined beauty and a clear feminine charm. Dia and Maha also possessed elite senses for beauty, but Dia was much more interested in collecting magic-related items, and Maha prioritized functionality over femininity.

I hadn't had the chance to view many chambers like this one.

If I had to make a comparison, I would've likened it to Mina's estate.

"Your praise honors me," Nevan responded. "Farron, bring us tea and sweets."

"Yes, Lady Nevan."

A tall female servant Nevan brought to the academy waited upon us both. A wonderful aroma rose from the tea she poured.

"That's a nice scent. I don't believe I've ever had this kind of tea before," I said.

I was confident in my knowledge of tea leaves because of my efforts selling them at Natural You, but I had never encountered this smell before.

"It's a tea leaf we procured from overseas. Natural You does not have exclusivity over international deals. Whoever controls the ocean controls business—we've been working on transoceanic travel for over a century with that belief in mind. We have built ships that can survive monsters and storms alike, and we have sacrificed many to find safe routes of passage," Nevan explained.

House Romalung produced the greatest humanity had to offer. It wasn't surprising that they would have that level of technology. It was also impressive that they had the foresight to know that trade would become the main battlefield of business.

"House Romalung continues to impress."

"There is one thing I just can't accept, however."

"What's that?"

"Natural You's boats. I believed the vessels that House Romalung spent decades building were the greatest in the world. They are made of steel rather than wood, to protect them from the monsters of the ocean, and they are mana-powered, enabling them to move at high speeds without relying on the wind. They're perfect."

They had made steel boats in a world of magic. That was a true breakthrough in technology.

"Then a simple merchant named Illig Balor comes along and constructs ships with the same concept but a superior design in a minuscule amount of time. Next, he somehow finds many of the safe and profitable sea routes that we discovered only after much failure and pain."

"I didn't know Natural You possessed such amazing boats." I feigned ignorance because Lugh Tuatha Dé had no connection to Natural You.

"That's not all. Every one of the onboard sailing tools is very advanced. Take the compass. Illig figured out how to hold the compass horizontal even when the ship was moving, keeping its readings accurate. He even discovered the concept of longitude and invented a tool called the sextant to measure it. His ships can accurately determine their location while on the ocean. Those astounding discoveries will surely change sea voyages forever. Illig Balor is no ordinary person."

"He's quite the inventor, and he has my respect."

"You speak as if this has nothing to do with you."

"One of my fiancées works for Natural You, but I don't know her boss. You've roused my curiosity, though. I'll ask Maha to introduce me to Illig Balor sometime."

"You're set on playing dumb, I see," Nevan replied with a telling smile. I grinned back.

...I'm surprised by this. Everything Nevan just mentioned— the new model magic ships, the invention of the dry compass,

sextants to measure longitude—was top-secret information I'd taken efforts to keep from leaking. All this technology was vital to maintaining Natural You's superiority in matters of commerce.

Many ships presently hauled cargo along the continent, but hardly any companies traded between continents like Natural You did. Attempting an intercontinental journey with the standard boats available to crews was paramount to suicide.

That was why Natural You was able to make a killing. Chocolate was a prime example of the advantage our ships gave us—no one other than Natural You could even obtain cacao.

"I'll find proof eventually," Nevan declared.

"I don't have a clue what you mean... Anyway, I doubt you called me here for idle chatter. Get to the point," I urged.

"Yes, you're right. Now..." Nevan's attitude changed from that of a friend to that of the daughter of Duke Romalung. The very air seemed to grow thicker. "By the name of House Romalung, one of the four major dukedoms, I order you to use your hidden Tuatha Dé blade for the sake of the Alvanian Kingdom. Remove the lesion that plagues this land."

"I will if the target is truly harmful to the country."

The Romalungs always used this exact wording when presenting a job, and the response I used was a stock response given by the Tuatha Dé. We used them in writing and in person, and they perfectly encapsulated our roles to the kingdom.

Standard procedure dictated that Nevan give information on the target next. Curiously, the young female servant Nevan addressed as Farron remained present. If she'd been an ordinary attendant, there was no way she would've been permitted to hear this.

Farron had a steady and vigilant demeanor. I could also tell she possessed extremely powerful mana. Judging by those two qualities, I figured she was likely a blood relative of House Romalung and a confidante of Nevan.

"The lesion we ask that you eliminate is the hierarch of the Alamite Church," Nevan announced.

"That explains why you had to give this job to me directly. On the very small chance this got out, we'd all be finished. We'd be enemies of the entire world," I responded.

"Goodness, I thought you'd be surprised."

"I am. However, I'd already considered this possibility."

"I am impressed by the reach of your ears."

Alamism was the official religion of nearly every country in the world, making it the most prominent religion. A shrine maiden called the Alam Karla held a high position in the church, and she helped the hero in her fight against the demons by sharing divine revelations.

Unlike the many shams in other religions who falsely claimed to hear the voice of a god, the Alam Karla was the real deal. The goddess had told me herself that she used the Alam Karla as a vessel through which to deliver her voice and manage the world. The documents on the hero and demons that the Alamite Church maintained were also completely accurate. Alamism was genuinely helping to save the world, which was why it had so many devoted followers.

"You are the only person in the world capable of this assassination. Will you take it on?"

"Tell me why the hierarch needs to die."

The regular reports from my information network that I'd spread throughout the country had led me to believe the church

was up to some suspicious activity. That knowledge alone didn't give me grounds for an assassination, however.

"A demon has taken the place of the hierarch, and the Alam Karla's life is in danger. Is that not enough reason to act? ...Oh my, *there* is the surprise I was looking for."

...*A demon has replaced the hierarch?!* If true, this was a massive problem. The demon could easily trap and kill the hero or the Alam Karla. Even worse, it could use the Alam Karla's status as the oracle and pass off its own decrees as the goddess's.

Plunging the world into chaos would be a piece of cake. The demon could also ruin my life. All it had to do was declare that the goddess had branded me evil. There was a good chance the demon would do so, as I'd vanquished several of its kin. I'd do the same thing if I were a demon.

People depended on society to live. No matter how strong someone was, only ruin awaited them if they made an enemy of the world. At the very least, I wouldn't be able to live as Lugh Tuatha Dé any longer.

"I accept."

The first thing to do would be to collect evidence. If I found enough to support Nevan's claim, I would kill the demon disguised as the hierarch as swiftly as possible.

"I greatly appreciate it."

This would be the most difficult assassination of my two lives. Killing a human hierarch would have been challenging enough, but this target was a powerful demon.

That wouldn't stop me, however. This job was necessary to protect my happiness and that of the people I loved.

My assassination target was the hierarch of the Alamite Church. I was already working on a number of plans in the back of my mind, and I continued to do so as I spoke. "I have two questions."

"Ask away. I will answer if I am able," Nevan responded.

"First, are you not going to inquire about the method of my assassination? Will you need me to conceal the hierarch's death as I did with the prince?"

I'd killed a prince of this kingdom not too long ago. His murder would've been a scandal, so I made his demise look like it was caused by an illness. I wouldn't have been surprised if Nevan imposed the same stipulation for the hierarch.

"All you have to do is kill him."

"Got it."

If I didn't have to hide that he was assassinated, the easiest way to get the job done would be to snipe him from long distance with a rifle. The hierarch often made public appearances to give speeches—I could get him then. If I made full use of all my magic techniques, I could snipe from a maximum range of two kilometers.

This world had no concept of long-distance sharpshooting. There would be guards in place to watch for archers, but a bow could only reach two to three hundred meters at best. No one would imagine that someone could be shot from kilometers away. As such, there would be no one monitoring sniping positions and no defenses to obstruct my line of fire. Putting a bullet through his head would be easy.

The problem is, that won't be enough to kill the hierarch if he's a demon. Demons couldn't be killed unless you destroyed their Crimson Hearts. Before we could do that, we needed to materialize the Crimson Heart using a spell I'd created called Demonkiller. The effective range of Demonkiller was twenty to thirty meters at best. Even if the roles of sniper and Demonkiller caster were divided among two people, the latter person would be caught immediately.

Dia would have to be the one to use Demonkiller. She was a talented mage, but her physical strength and close combat capability left a little to be desired, and fleeing after the demon was killed would be nearly impossible for her.

I needed to think of something.

"What is your second question?" Nevan asked.

"How did you discover that the hierarch is a demon?"

"Now that is an inquiry I didn't expect."

"I think it's an obvious one."

"Yes, but you aren't going to take my word for it, are you? I expect you will do your own research."

Nevan understood me well. Whatever she told me, I was going to search for the truth using my own eyes and ears.

"There's a high chance that the reason House Romalung believes him to be a demon will be useful information and will make verifying this easier," I explained.

"You have a point. The answer is simple: The Alam Karla asked me for help."

If the claim originated from the goddess's oracle herself, then the hierarch almost certainly was a demon.

"...How did you receive the Alam Karla's SOS without being discovered by the hierarch?"

"I did not meet her as myself, but rather as Princess Farina's body double. Royal families from countries that practice Alamism regularly visit the Alam Karla to receive the word of the goddess."

In addition to being a daughter of House Romalung, Nevan was a body double for Farina, a princess of Alvan.

"That makes sense, but if the demon realizes that the Alam Karla knows the truth, it'll kill her. She has to realize that. I don't see why she would risk her life by telling you."

"I did not gain her trust overnight. I have spent years winning my way into her good graces because I thought I could use her. I am also certain she chose to confide in me largely because I am from the same country as the man who killed three demons... The Alam Karla believes you will save her, Sir Lugh."

Nevan was shrewd. This was also good news—the Alam Karla was aware of the hierarch's true identity and was my ally. If she was yet to fall into the demon's hands, that opened several options to me. The demon wouldn't be able to label me an enemy of the gods so easily.

However, the demon could easily replace the Alam Karla with an imposter.

"That's good to know. I'll work on a plan to protect her and find a way to meet with the hierarch. I've confronted multiple demons. No matter how well it conceals its true identity, I'll be able to tell if it's a demon or not if I see him in person... I'd like to meet him as Lugh Tuatha Dé, but that would be difficult."

We had circumstantial evidence, but I still couldn't be certain.

For that reason, I wanted to see the hierarch with my own two eyes.

"No, it will not. You defeated another demon, didn't you? Excluding the one the hero slew, you have killed the beetle, the lion, and now a third. The hierarch himself is saying that he is going to invite you to the Holy Land and lavish you with praise for your accomplishments. It seems he wants to invite your entire class and the class president as well."

Well, that's convenient... Too convenient.

"It's obviously a trap. I'm even gifting him hostages in the form of my classmates," I remarked.

"That is likely, given the timing of the summons. Is this not thrilling? We're in a battle of wits between human and demon."

Nevan wasn't wrong. It was clear that the Alam Karla held the key to this game of deception. If the hierarch proclaimed me an enemy of the goddess, nothing would come of it if the Alam Karla responded by saying I was innocent and denounced the hierarch as a demon. Conversely, if I didn't take measures before the Alam Karla fell into the demon's hands, it could use her role as the oracle to ostracize me from society.

I returned to my apartment and gave Dia and Tarte the gist of the situation. Now that I had accepted this job, I needed their assistance.

"Are you serious? The hierarch is a demon?! The world is doomed," exclaimed Dia.

With clear despair, Tarte muttered, "I can't believe the person closest in the world to the divine is a demon in disguise..."

"We have a precedent for this, remember? The snake demon Mina infiltrated noble society in much the same way. It's not a leap to assume that another could slip into the church," I pointed out.

Demons were much more than just strong monsters. That was what made them so difficult to deal with.

"Do you have a plan? This is really, really bad. You made it sound like we're finished if the Alam Karla is already under the demon's control," Dia said.

"That's why I'm going to act one step ahead. I highly doubt the demon has accounted for my aircraft. I'll sneak away as soon as we get out of class tomorrow," I explained.

"This isn't the time to worry about classes!" Dia shouted.

I wished that were the case. This was a battle against time; it would be best if I could skip class and depart as quickly as possible.

"You would think. The problem is, there's someone in our class with a connection to the demons. If I do anything conspicuous, there's a chance word of it could reach the demon posing as the hierarch," I pointed out.

"You mean Lord Naoise... Um, aren't the demons supposed to be competing against each other?" asked Tarte.

"Mina has been acting suspiciously since the earth dragon demon appeared. At the very least, she hasn't done enough to earn my trust."

I had a pretty good idea of what Mina was plotting. She loved human society and culture and wanted to eliminate the other demons that would destroy it. That much was true. However, I also had reason to suspect she wanted to obtain the power of the Demon King. To achieve that, she required at least three Fruits of Life, each of which was made from over ten thousand human souls.

Mina knew she would become a target of mine if she tried to make a Fruit of Life herself. Thus, she'd chosen to let the other demons do the work for her and then steal the fruits. However, only four demons remained, including Mina. She didn't expect there'd only be a single Fruit of Life this late into the game, and she wouldn't welcome the death of another demon.

"That's true. So what will you do when you meet with the Alam Karla?" Dia inquired.

"Make sure she isn't already under the demon's control," I said.

Although a true oracle, the Alam Karla was still an ordinary human. A demon would have no trouble brainwashing her. She'd be incapable of defending herself.

Nervously, Dia wondered aloud, "What if she's already fallen under the demon's sway?"

"I'd be finished. Ostracization from society would be inevitable. I would throw away my name and run."

That was how enormous Alamism's influence was. Its enemy was the enemy of every person in the nation. People would curse me as a devil and hurl stones at me as I walked down the street. Living as Lugh Tuatha Dé would be impossible.

I could exist as Illig Balor or move to a faraway land beyond the reach of the church. Either way, I'd have to live under a different identity while searching for a chance to clear my name.

"I'll go with you if it comes to that," Dia declared.

"Me too!" Tarte agreed.

"You do realize we'll be treated as significantly worse than criminals?" I responded.

"I do. But that's preferable to being apart from you," Dia insisted.

"I am your personal retainer, my lord! I will follow you any-where!" Tarte cried.

Their straightforward affection deeply moved me.

"Thank you. I'm happy to hear that. Please accompany me if that time comes. I'd be lonely without you both."

"Heh-heh, you can count on us."

"I'd never let you be alone, my lord."

I was really glad I had bound myself to these girls. We smiled at each other, then, feeling a little awkward, I cleared my throat. Dia and Tarte looked a little bashful, too, but fortunately, Dia got us back on topic.

"So what will you do if the Alam Karla isn't under the demon's control yet?"

"I'll abduct and shelter her. If we have the Alam Karla, noth-ing the hierarch says will have any sway. The goddess chooses the Alam Karla, and the hierarch is just a position created by humans," I said with a reassuring smile. Obtaining the Alam Karla would give us an instant advantage. I could even get her to announce that the hierarch was a demon.

"…U-um, so basically you'll go to the Holy Land, sneak into the cathedral—the most heavily guarded place in the world—grab the Alam Karla, and escape. All while keeping your identity hidden," Tarte summarized.

Dia frowned. "Is that possible?"

"I'll pull it off. I have to. I mean, afterward I'll have to deal with the impossibly difficult mission of assassinating a demon that has disguised himself as the hierarch. If I can't do a little rescue mission first, I'm screwed."

Rescuing the Alam Karla would be difficult, but I could get

it done. I was going to start by using my telecommunications network to prepare resources and a safe house to protect the oracle, and to get myself ready for the trip.

This was a battle against time, and I'd operate as swiftly as I could without panicking. It had been a while since I'd exercised my assassin's intellect. I was going to succeed perfectly.

I left the academy as soon as class ended. There was no unusual behavior from Naoise. He actually treated me as a normal friend, as though things were no different from how they were before the orc demon attack.

I left the school grounds, then disguised myself and took off into the skies using my aircraft. My current goal was to secure the Alam Karla. If I was caught, not even rank as a Holy Knight would prevent my entire family from being sentenced to death. It wouldn't stop with my family, either; the entire Alvanian Kingdom would fall under threat from the church. That's why I disguised myself.

I had to accept this mission, regardless of the danger, because I was toast if I didn't. Our chances of overcoming this situation would improve dramatically if I could secure the Alam Karla before the enemy acted.

Jobs like this would be much easier if I had a body double. I'd become too famous. Circumstances had arisen that made that fame necessary, but I'd still become too accomplished and garnered more attention than I would've liked. That made it challenging to perform my job. Given this, I felt a strong need for another self.

If I'd had a body double today, I could have sent him to class in my place, enabling me to depart last night.

Unfortunately, finding a suitable person has been difficult.

I could use makeup to change his appearance, but his natural facial features and his body build had to be close enough to mine.

The biggest obstacle was that the person needed to be a mage. Unless they were intentionally hiding it, mages always leaked mana. I couldn't expect anyone to have my mana capacity, but if my body double didn't possess a certain amount of magical power, people would realize something was off. To make matters worse, almost all mages were nobles, and not many would be willing to serve as my double.

Ideally, I would've liked a person talented enough to participate convincingly in Class S, but I gave up on that immediately.

"I'll have to make something work."

Depending on how things developed from here, things might be hopeless without a replacement for myself.

I traveled a great distance with my aircraft and arrived in the Holy Land, where the Alam Karla lived. The name of the land was Fomoire. It was simultaneously a small city and a country, making it the tiniest nation in the world. The royal capital had a Sanctuary located underneath it, but this entire city was considered sacred.

Nearly all towns had walls to keep out monsters, but not this one. Instead, it had a barrier of an absurd scale that covered the entire settlement. Its scale and strength were beyond what any human could manage and had been created by the power of the gods. The barrier was said to eliminate all impurity and was supposedly harmless to humans but lethal to monsters.

"...There's more to it than that." I observed the divine barrier from a distance and quickly deduced the formula using my Tuatha Dé eyes.

Dia and I had spent over a decade analyzing the rules of magic, and I understood most of the code used to write formulas. Despite that, I could only read about 60 percent of the barrier's formula. The magic we understood was a power the gods had simplified for human use. This was a spell used by the gods themselves. The peculiar code was on a whole other level of complexity.

I didn't shy away from the challenge, though. *A divine barrier... This is good study. I'd like to show this to Dia.* Taking the parts of the magical equation I could comprehend, I formed a number of hypotheses, chose the one with the highest level of consistency, and began making some guesses.

"I get the gist of it... That's no simple barrier. It's an information management system. It looks like there's a hole, though."

The barrier managed information. I was surprised to see that it scanned mana wavelengths and identified individuals. Its manager could track every person who entered or exited the city.

I would be able to pass through because it was specialized to keep out monsters, but the barrier's manager would know that someone entered without permission. *They wouldn't know it was me, but it would still put them on guard.* I'd never been to this city, so there was no way they could know my mana wavelength. I wouldn't be identified.

That said, I feared that the hierarch would assume that any unidentified intruder was me. If the hierarch were indeed a demon, it'd be on the lookout for me because I'd killed three of its kind. Most people wouldn't do something as reckless as sneak into the Holy Land, which would lead the demon to assume I was the intruder.

I considered the option of destroying the barrier. Modifying it would be impossible, because I only understood 60 percent of the formula, but I thought I could meddle with the code and break it. Doing so would require me to use the third arm divine treasure I'd brought along. It was very effective as a weapon, but its true value was its nature as the hand of a god—it allowed me to touch things human hands couldn't.

I can destroy it. But that would be a bad move. If I was worried about putting the hierarch on guard just by passing through the barrier without permission, it made no sense to do something as brash as eliminating the barrier. I rejected the idea.

I only had one real option. "I'll throw myself over the barrier." The field surrounded the city and extended about ten kilometers above and below the ground. It wasn't a dome but a high wall. The top was undefended.

The assumption was likely that would-be intruders with wings would never ascend to the ridiculous height of ten kilometers above the earth. An elite mage using wind magic couldn't reach that high.

Even for me, it was impossible to fly over the barrier with wind and physical strengthening. Fortunately, I had a third option.

I started by surrounding myself with wind. It wasn't for flying but for protection. As for my method of going up...

"God Spear, *Gungnir!*"

The deadly spell I'd created fired objects to a high altitude by reversing gravity around them. I'd originally designed this magic as a physics-based weapon of mass destruction. I could also use it to send enemies themselves flying into the air.

If I used the spell on myself, however, I could fly with great efficiency. I couldn't afford a moment of carelessness, though. I was flinging myself into the sky to fall back down, and my speed was going to increase by 9.8 meters per second. That tremendously fast rate would place a massive burden on my body, and maintaining control of my magic while moving that swiftly would be challenging. If I lost consciousness during the spell, I would fall to the ground and die on impact.

I couldn't believe merely entering the city undetected demanded this much effort. I had to laugh as I completed the spell.

My face stiffened as I began to accelerate. My speed grew exponentially as I rose into the sky to eventually fall.

I ended the spell according to my calculations, but I continued to rise. I used kinetic energy to decelerate as I climbed higher and higher into the sky. When I crossed over the Holy Land's barrier completely, I used the rest of my kinetic energy to bring myself to a full stop, then allowed gravity to drag me down.

The air was thin and cold. Air pressure and temperature dropped at high altitudes, and oxygen became scarce. Furthermore, the more sudden the shift in pressure and temperature, the greater the burden on the body.

Even Mount Everest was only eight kilometers tall. When you considered how many people had collapsed from declining air pressure while climbing that peak, hurtling your body ten kilometers into the sky at high speed could only be judged suicidal. Had I not covered myself with wind magic for protection, I would've perished.

I gathered wind via a spell and used it to thrust myself directly above the Holy Land. Then I used that same magic to reverse thrust and prevent myself from descending too quickly. Once I reached a low enough elevation, I discarded the spell to protect myself and replaced it with one that created a thin layer of air that refracted light. This was a special ability of mine to make myself invisible.

I strengthened my reverse thrusting as I approached the ground and brought myself to a near halt. By using my entire body to absorb the impact, I landed safely and as quietly as possible. I immediately rushed into a back alley, and after confirming there was no one around, I dispelled my invisibility.

I had infiltrated the city undetected.

"The first phase is clear. On to the main mission." I stared at the cathedral located in the center of the Holy Land. That was where the Alam Karla waited.

I'd looked into her schedule beforehand. What I heard from my intelligence network was consistent with what Nevan told me, so my information was very reliable.

One hour from now, the Alam Karla would perform her weekly purification ritual in the cathedral's bathhouse. The holy water of the bath enhanced her power as the oracle. No one accompanied her into the bathhouse—not one guard or attendant. She was practically begging someone to kidnap her.

If I missed this opportunity, there was no guarantee I'd find her alone again. That was why I couldn't afford to alert the demon to my presence. If it upped security, any hope of finding the Alam Karla alone would vanish.

I blended into the city and slipped into a crowd headed for the cathedral. I was an assassin, not a kidnapper, but I wasn't going to get upset that this mission demanded I operate a little differently. Being an assassin demanded versatility.

I infiltrated the cathedral after avoiding an array of traps. In contrast to the strict defenses around the great temple, the interior was totally defenseless. I didn't let myself get comfortable, though. I kept my Tuatha Dé eyes active to look out for magical ploys, while simultaneously using my assassin's skill of observation to scan for physical ones. From here on, losing focus for a moment could mean forfeiting my life.

I saw my reflection in a mirror on the way and chuckled to myself. *I had no choice, but I still can't believe I'm wearing this kind of disguise again.* Upon reaching the cathedral, I'd disguised myself as a nun. They were the only ones who could enter the section of the cathedral where the Alam Karla lived.

Fortunately, Alamite nuns wore loose skirts, meaning I could bend my knees slightly as I walked, to make myself appear shorter. The thin veil on my hat was convenient as well. It was unlikely anyone would realize my gender with my face concealed, and even if someone did see my face, no one would think twice about not recognizing me.

I followed the diagram of the cathedral Nevan gave me and headed for my destination, the bathhouse. It was the only place the Alam Karla would be alone.

Spying a plump man ahead of me, I moved against the wall

and bowed in the Alamism style. Men were prohibited from this part of the cathedral, but I guessed from his clothes that he was a high priest. Something about him seemed vulgar, though. Rather than pass by, he made straight for me.

He couldn't have noticed I'm not a real nun, could he?

"Show me your face, sister," the man said. I obeyed and lifted my veil. "Hmm... You're beautiful, but I wish you were younger. That's enough. Carry on."

"Understood."

Having lost interest, the high priest walked away.

Looks like Alamism was unable to escape the corruption of society. I understood what kind of man he was the moment I saw his lust-filled eyes. He undoubtedly came here looking for nuns to play with every day.

Perhaps this baseness resulted from the hierarch being a demon, but I doubted it. Religion always gathered money and power, which corrupted people and drew in bad characters. As far as I knew, no matter how commendable the doctrine, things always ended up like this once it got big. I had seen that many times in my previous life, and I'd received many jobs asking me to assassinate people who had given in to lust.

Good thing I took care with the disguise. I didn't have a great need to alter my face because I was going to be wearing a veil, but my caution had been warranted. Had my face been to his liking, he could have dragged me back to his room; that would have been trouble.

I was almost at my destination. I needed to remain focused until the job was done.

After gathering information on the way and confirming that the Alam Karla was about to take her bath, I hid above the ceiling of the bathhouse. I was going to wait there until she arrived. A probing wind spell provided me with an understanding of the situation below. I felt a pang of guilt for what was functionally peeping on the Alam Karla in the bath, but this was the only chance to find her alone.

It was nearly time for the Alam Karla's bath, according to Nevan's intel. I heard footsteps, and then the person I was waiting for appeared. Her hair, skin, and every other feature were all pale. She was wearing thin clothing that stuck to her skin. I'd thought this the first time I saw her, but it still surprised me how much she resembled the goddess.

I held my breath and kept quiet while descending through the hidden door I'd made in the ceiling. I approached my target from a blind spot, then grabbed her from behind and put a hand over her mouth.

"*Hmmm, hmmm!*"

The Alam Karla panicked and struggled, but she could barely move. I was using a professional restraining technique. She would have screamed if I'd appeared before her in the bathhouse without warning, which would have caused a disturbance. That was why I chose to grab her.

I whispered in her ear. "It's Lugh Tuatha Dé. I came here to save you on Princess Farina's request."

She calmed down at those words. I used Princess Farina's name because Nevan had spoken to the Alam Karla while disguised as the princess.

"I'm about to release you. Keep quiet so that your attendants outside won't hear," I instructed.

The Alam Karla nodded. I let her go once I was confident she'd calmed down.

"Thank you for coming to save me," she said softly. Strangely enough, she was carrying a makeup kit, which included lipstick, something that suited my plan perfectly. Using the Alam Karla's would be far more natural than using what I'd brought.

"You can thank me later. We have to get out of here first. Before we leave, I want you to use your lipstick to write what I say on the wall."

"Um, why do you want me to do that?"

"There's no time. I'll explain later. This is what I want you to write: 'I am going to the goddess's side.'" The young woman gave a puzzled expression, but she obeyed.

This was a cheap trick, but it served me better if people thought the Alam Karla had disappeared because of the goddess rather than because of kidnapping. I didn't want anyone searching for her and her abductor. Plus, being kidnapped would harm her reputation. My preparations would ensure that the rumor of her miraculous disappearance would be picked up by the nuns and spread throughout the cathedral and beyond.

"Okay, let's go. Grab on to me tightly."

I hugged the Alam Karla close, then rode on wind to return to the ceiling. Her white hair came loose from her head as we ascended—a wig. Red locks spilled out from beneath.

Shoot, is she a body double for the real Alam Karla? Thankfully, that wasn't the case. I could tell she was the genuine article because she possessed the same aura of the goddess that I had. Maybe she trusted me because she recognized that, too.

The Alam Karla fought hard to keep her wig from flying away, and there was another thing wrong as well. Something white was rubbing off onto my clothes from the touch of her skin. Her skin was fake, just like her hair. I was curious about it, but this wasn't the time for questions.

I climbed through the hidden door I'd used to get into the bathhouse, closed it tight, then hurried into a vent and onto the roof. From there, I used a route I'd confirmed was safe beforehand and headed for our hideout.

The refuge I'd prepared was a building in the Holy Land, a safe house obtained using resources from Natural You. I'd purchased the house under a false identity and possessed others like it in several major cities.

I served the Alam Karla an herbal tea with a relaxing effect to help her calm down.

"We have a lot to discuss. Where should I start...?" I said.

"...Are you not going to ask about my hair and skin?" she questioned.

"Let's start there."

The Alam Karla removed her false hair and began to remove the white paint on her skin. She was a redhead, and while her skin was fair, it was a human color rather than the inhuman alabaster of the goddess. I'd judged her to be a woman in her twenties when we last met, but without her disguise, she seemed no older than her late teens. Makeup could completely change how a person was perceived.

"The Alam Karla is the mouthpiece of the goddess Venus, and

she is required to have her white skin. All the Alam Karlas before me were obligated to paint their bodies as well... Only the hierarch and a handful of other people know about this."

"That explains why you enter the bathhouse alone."

People in high stations often brought attendants into the bathhouse to serve them. The Alam Karla was one of the most important people in the world, and you'd think she'd want guards by her side at all times.

"The bathhouse is the only place I ever get to set the Alam Karla aside and become Myrrha again."

"If people aren't supposed to know you wear makeup, it might have been a mistake to have you write the message in lipstick."

"No, lipstick is fine. The powder is a secret, but I don't hide the lipstick at all. No one thinks that the shade of my lipstick is my natural color."

She probably carried around lipstick to distract people from the powder she used to color her skin white. The Alam Karla applied common, everyday makeup in the bath as a kind of distraction. No one could be allowed to realize that she disguised her skin, but freshly applied powder had a particular scent. That smell could be explained if people knew that she donned other makeup in the bath.

"You have it rough," I said.

"I knew what I was getting into when I assumed the position. All I have to do is listen to the goddess's voice and convey it, and I'm able to live a good life," she responded.

I inferred from her words and attitude that she was not born into a family of high social status. She was only given this position because she was an oracle. Her life was all thanks to the goddess

judging her compatible. I'd felt a detached sense from the Alam Karla the first time we met, but the girl before me now looked as normal as could be.

"I see… I assume you have a reason important enough to risk that position by seeking help."

"Yes, I do. I'm going to be killed if nothing is done. You will be, too."

"Me too, huh? Princess Farina told me that a demon has taken the place of the hierarch. How do you know about it?"

That was my single biggest doubt about this situation. If the Alam Karla possessed some ability to see through demons' disguises, I could believe her, but that felt unlikely. She was only an ordinary person who could hear the goddess's voice. However imperfect his disguise, the demon was able to become the hierarch of the Alamite Church and fool all of the highest-ranking clergy members in the world. His methods of concealment had to be top-notch. It was unthinkable that this girl was the only one to see through that facade.

I was skeptical of her ability to gather intelligence as well. Speaking with her made it plain that she was an ordinary young woman.

"…Well, because Venus used my body to speak to the hierarch—the demon. I was conscious during the conversation, and I remember what they said."

I was speechless. The goddess spoke directly to a demon? I had a bad feeling about this.

Is she in league with the demon? I wondered. It wasn't impossible. The goddess's purpose was to preserve the world. She didn't exist to support humanity but to support the world itself. I'd collected information to suggest that while demons were the enemy of people, they were not a danger to the planet. Thus, the goddess could join hands with one.

"I'd like for you to repeat to me what they said," I requested.

This was a stroke of fortune, in a way. Had I not been here, I wouldn't have learned of the goddess's conversation with a demon.

Were it true that the goddess used the Alam Karla to speak with the demon disguised as the hierarch, it'd be too critical to ignore.

Just as the Alam Karla was about to recount the story, her stomach growled.

"S-sorry. This is hardly the time for that...," she said, holding her gut in embarrassment.

"Let's have a light meal first. I'll cook something. Do you have any foods you can't eat?" I asked.

This was likely to be a long talk, so it was best to allow her to eat first. I needed to hear what she had to say, but gaining her trust was crucial, too. I didn't want to push her too hard. Logically, she'd understand that the conversation was more important than her hunger, but it'd still leave her displeased. The heart did not follow reason.

"I can't make you wait," the girl replied.

"I'm hungry as well. Don't worry about it."

"Really? That would be great, then."

"I've prepared the room over there for you. There's a change of clothes ready, since I doubt you'll be able to relax in that outfit. Feel free to change and rest until the food is ready."

The Alam Karla looked down at what she was wearing. She

was still in the thin dress that she'd donned for the purification ritual in the bathhouse.

"Th-thank you. I'll be waiting there, then. Also, I can't eat fish," she said with a nod, and she walked into her room.

Thirty minutes later, I finished cooking and called the Alam Karla back. Her complexion looked much improved; she must have taken a nap. She'd changed into loose loungewear. Without her wig and makeup, she seemed like a completely different person.

"Here you are. Dig in," I said as I set pancakes and hot chocolate on the table.

"Thank you very much. Wow, this is so sweet. The black drink is amazing. It warms you right up," she praised.

"That's called hot chocolate. It's a special drink of mine."

"It's so, so good."

"I'll make more for you, then. You'll be living in hiding for the next few days, after all."

Hot chocolate calmed the mind and was very nutritional. It was the perfect drink for her right now.

"Is it okay for me to use this house?"

"This is the safest place for you. People I trust will deliver you supplies at regular intervals. You shouldn't want for anything."

The Alam Karla had work left to do in the Holy Land, and considering how I would be taking her in and out of this city, keeping her in a safe house carried the least risk. I explained that to her as we ate, and she nodded.

"I'm sorry for all the trouble I'm putting you through.

Wow, these pancakes are incredible. They're so light and fluffy; they're the best I've ever eaten."

This girl was one of the most important people in the world, but I didn't feel that gravitas from her as she ate.

"I used a little trick of mine."

The baking powder used to make bread and cakes rise didn't exist in this world, but Natural You had just developed it. I kneaded baking powder and yogurt into the pancakes and went easy on the oil. That resulted in airy dough. Even someone who felt weak could enjoy a fluffy pancake.

I watched as she finished the pancakes and hot chocolate.

"Thank you for the food. I wouldn't have thought such a delicious meal could be made on the run. You're a good cook, Sir Lugh."

"It's a hobby. You're looking much better already... Can we return to our conversation? What did the goddess say when she used your body to meet with the demon?"

"Honestly, I remember what they said, but I don't know what Venus meant by any of it," the Alam Karla replied, hanging her head apologetically.

"That's good enough. Just tell me exactly what you heard."

The girl's own interpretations would only be a needless distraction. I could also imagine that the goddess used some intentionally strange phraseology, so it was best to hear her statement precisely.

"Okay, this is what Venus said: 'I won't interfere with you, so you don't interfere with me. The promised day we have been eagerly awaiting is almost here. This hero is not being depleted enough.' That's all."

"How did the demon respond?"

"He accepted the goddess's proposal and said that he'd take measures regarding the hero... Then he demanded that the goddess abide by their neutrality."

"Neutrality... That's an interesting word. That's how the demon sees Venus. Not as an enemy or an ally, but as a bystander."

There were several things about the goddess's statement that bothered me. What did she mean by "interfere"? What about the "promised day"? From the demons' perspective, that could mean the resurrection of the Demon King, but I didn't know why the goddess would look forward to that. And what about that comment regarding the hero being insufficiently depleted? That was likely due to me fighting demons in Epona's place. The wording made the hero sound like a basic consumable.

It was also worth noting that the goddess was *criticizing* the lack of depletion. There was no way power that great didn't come with a cost. I was interested to know what happened after depletion. If Epona lacked a high mana recovery rate like me and only possessed overwhelming instantaneous discharge without the ability to regain the strength she exerted, it'd be a valuable bit of knowledge in the event that I chose to kill her.

I'd need to do my best to gather more detailed information on those matters later.

"Thank you. That was helpful," I said.

"I'm glad to hear it," the Alam Karla responded.

"There's one more thing I don't understand. Why did you say that you feared for your life? Nothing that Venus and the demon said suggested that your life is in danger."

That conversation never involved the Alam Karla.

"The hierarch has been threatening me even before I learned

that he is a demon. He demanded I convey his words to the people as the goddess's. He threatened to kill me if I disobeyed, saying he'd find an Alam Karla who'd listen. I remained steadfast in my refusal and prayed for Venus's aid. But she did nothing to help!"

In all probability, the goddess had no interest in the Alam Karla, or rather, in the girl named Myrrha. There were plenty of viable replacements. The goddess was functionally a mechanism to maintain the world; she had no emotional attachment to individuals. That applied to me as well. If the goddess found someone more useful, she'd abandon me without a second thought.

"She didn't mention me when she talked to the demon, either... That was when I realized Venus would not save me. Yesterday, the hierarch killed one of my attendants and said that I was next... So I gave in. I spoke the demon's words as the those of the goddess this morning." Myrrha began to cry.

I'd been just barely too late.

"What did you say?"

"I stated in front of everyone that the goddess has never spoken to you. I was scared. I didn't want to die, or worse, lose my status as the Alam Karla... I can't go back to my old life. I don't want to be miserable scum again. I'm sorry. I'm so sorry..."

Myrrha hugged herself as tears streamed down her face. Her nails dug into her skin, scratching off white dye that didn't come away earlier.

"You've done well to make it this far," I assured her.

"Aren't you mad? I ruined you out of fear for my own life."

She was right about that. The demon had prepared a trap by summoning me to the Holy Land and then having the Alam Karla denounce my connection to the goddess. I'd already fallen from my place of reverence in society to a despicable person who'd misappropriated the goddess's name. My inquisition would undoubtedly begin the moment I officially arrived in the Holy Land.

"It's not your fault; it's the demon's. It forced you into it."

"Even still, I…"

"If you feel guilt, lend me your hand. I plan to charge right into the demon's trap. I'm going to attend the trial."

I was going to break through the demon's trap head-on.

"That's suicide. It's a trial only in name. You *will* be convicted, and they don't intend to listen to your argument at all."

Naturally, I was aware of that. That's how religion worked. People in power placed great importance on their images, and that tendency was even stronger in religious leaders. One of them would never admit a mistake, nor could they afford to. Guilt was decided the moment an accusation was made. Those blamed had to be guilty, or the leader's credibility would take a hit.

That didn't just apply to the hierarch; everyone involved in the inquisition would feel the same way. I had no chance of winning, no matter how well I defended myself.

"Typically, you'd be right. But my defense will be anything but typical. If I have the aid of the goddess's true representative, I can win. I guarantee you that the hierarch has already prepared your successor. You're not the Alam Karla any longer. The church will make no attempts to rescue you. In fact, they'll likely send an assassin."

It suited the demon better to find a new Alam Karla than to deal with a troublesome old one. Whether she could hear the goddess's voice or not didn't actually matter to the church. The hierarch could appoint any puppet, and the people would accept it as long as he claimed she was an oracle. None could confirm it other than the Alam Karla herself, after all.

"Huh? I—I..."

Myrrha probably hadn't thought that far ahead when she fled with me. She never doubted her own value and overestimated what it meant that she heard the goddess's voice. If she'd known things would turn out like this, she might have rejected my help.

I was cornering her this way on purpose. I'd come to realize through our conversation that the Alam Karla was a very headstrong person. She apologized for causing me trouble, but she didn't show a hint of guilt until doing so. If she were indeed the tenderhearted young woman she appeared to be, she would have felt shame the moment she saw me, and it would have shown in her behavior.

And yet, I detected no remorse until after her apology. That was proof that she was putting on a performance. Her guilt was a calculated attempt to win my sympathy and forgiveness.

"You tried to protect me after being threatened with death. I couldn't ask for more," I said with a smile. Despite everything I'd realized about Myrrha, I pretended that her act had achieved the desired effect.

It was worth noting that Myrrha hadn't first refused to give the false message for my sake. She did so to protect her value as the goddess's oracle. She knew instinctively that the Alam Karla's worth declined every time she lied, and she was also afraid of displeasing her patron deity.

Lying was easy, yet the moment she did so, the role of the Alam Karla became a position that anyone in the world could fill. The nature of the job required Myrrha to continue delivering the goddess's words genuinely.

That means she is driven by self-interest. My best bet at convincing her was not by appealing with emotion, but rather by showing how my plan would benefit her. I needed to tell her that I would eliminate the hierarch, who had become an obstacle for her, and create an environment that enabled her to maintain her position as the Alam Karla.

So that was what I was doing. This kind of person was very easy to handle.

"If you want to be the Alam Karla again, your only option is to attend the inquisition with me and take down the impostor in the hierarch's place. I've made all the necessary preparations to make that happen."

It was problematic that the Alam Karla had already denounced me, but I'd accounted for that scenario. I had a way to strike back, and I'd laid the necessary groundwork for a counter.

"Very well. I will fight. Both to atone for my sins and for myself... I really do want to remain the Alam Karla."

That surprised me. I didn't expect Myrrha to voice her true motivations.

I smiled kindly and put my hands on her shoulders. "That's the resolve I want to see. Let's do this together."

"Okay!"

It would have been ill-advised even for me to defend myself at the inquisition without the genuine Alam Karla at hand. I was glad I had gained her cooperation. This increased my options significantly.

The first phase of my plan was to spread a rumor that the goddess took the Alam Karla. I wanted people to think the gossip originated with her attendants. That message left in lipstick was our lifeline. Without it, I likely would've been saddled with the crime of killing the Alam Karla.

Hopefully, Nevan was taking care of the job I'd tasked her

with. I couldn't believe she could sneak intelligence agents into the cathedral. House Romalung never ceased to amaze. It would've been impossible to abduct the Alam Karla and spread word of the message before it was erased without their assistance.

In a sense, this was a battle. I was going to treat it like an all-out war.

After securing the Alam Karla in the safe house and instructing her not to go outside, I returned to the academy. The moon shone brightly in the night sky when I landed on the roof of my dorm. After confirming that I hadn't been seen, I returned to my apartment through the window.

I then grabbed my study materials and got ready to depart. I was going to participate in our weekly study group. I'd originally started it to help Epona lift her poor grades, but now, nearly everyone in Class S participated.

Attending would give me an alibi. The concept of aircraft didn't exist in this world. There was no way anyone could believe that I'd made a round trip to the Holy Land and back in just half a day. Even with Epona's physical strength, it was impossible. At the very least, I wouldn't be suspected of kidnapping the Alam Karla.

Epona called out to me the next day after class. She was the hero the goddess said would eventually destroy the world and was the person I was reincarnated to kill. Despite that, I was searching for a way to save everyone without having to take her life.

As always, she was wearing a male uniform and presenting as

male. She only looked like a handsome young boy to me, but she had nice facial features, and I would have liked to see her as a girl.

I smiled at her. "What's going on? Is everything okay?"

I'd initially approached Epona out of calculated self-interest to gain information about the hero and to ingratiate myself to her so that she'd let her guard down when I had to kill her. Now, though, I thought of her as a true companion.

"I don't want to hide anything from a friend, so I'll give it to you straight. This morning, some people from the church told me that you've been passing off your own words as the goddess's and trying to throw the world into chaos. They told me many more bad things about you, too. They said it's a lie that you are being invited to the Holy Land for commendation on defeating demons and that you're actually going to be tried. I was given an order to keep watch over you so you don't run, and to stop you by force if you try."

The church moves fast. According to the Alam Karla, it was yesterday morning that she'd declared that the goddess didn't speak to me. A carrier pigeon with orders for church members at the academy would've been too slow. They must have had this plan ready for some time.

This demon was quite intelligent. It was trying to deal with me using Epona and expend her energy by having her fight me. Nothing could serve it better than simultaneously eliminating the biggest threat to its plans and depleting the hero.

"I was honest with you, so I want you to be honest with me. Have you been lying?" asked Epona.

"No. The church is," I answered.

Epona's expression softened at my answer, and she let out a huge sigh. "That's a relief. That means I can proudly support you."

"I'm glad you trust me, but should you really do so that easily?"

Epona smiled and nodded. "You saved me. I would've been out of the fight for good if not for you. You've already killed multiple demons and saved so many lives. I trust you significantly more than those arrogant people in the cathedral. If you say you've been telling the truth, then that's good enough for me."

I grinned wryly. For better or worse, Epona had not been tainted by the church. Alamism was the world's religion, and its influence was immense. No one could criticize the church, no matter how wrong its declarations were. Even a noble jeopardized their standing by speaking against the organization. People who took that into account were better off.

Those who had the belief instilled in them at a young age that the teachings of Alamism were infallible and never questioned otherwise were the worst kind of people. They didn't listen to logic, and words couldn't reach them. That was the problem with religion; it moved people with emotion rather than reason.

"Thank you for believing me. Having you as an enemy is a terrifying thought," I said. I was still incapable of defeating Epona in a fair fight. I wasn't even sure I'd be able to escape.

Man, the church is extraordinarily powerful. The pigs in the royal capital had shackled Epona to their city out of fear for their own lives. That was why I'd been named a Holy Knight and tasked with the job of racing about the kingdom to deal with the demons. Despite that, Epona was being sent to the Holy Land now. That was proof that the church's authority overrode the government's desire for self-preservation. The church would make for a powerful enemy.

"You can't relax yet, Lugh. You still have the inquisition! What should we do? Should I, um, help you flee?" Epona offered.

"You don't have to do anything. I'm going to attend the hearing. I'll clear my name of all charges by the book," I answered.

The trial was going to attract a lot of attention. If I ran, I would never be able to remove the church's accusations.

"Are you sure you can do that?"

Even Epona, as green as she was, knew what an inquisition meant. It wasn't a real proceeding meant for discussion and finding the truth; it was a stage to convict and shame people in public view.

"I can. But just in case, will you rescue me if it looks like I'm about to be killed?"

"Of course I will."

"...You know that helping me will make you an enemy of the world, right?" I asked, feeling a little concern for Epona. If she was underestimating the power of the Alamite Church, I needed to give her a firm education. Using her by taking advantage of her ignorance was not something a friend would do.

"I know that. But I have to protect my friends...and you need to uphold your promise. You said you'd kill me if I ever lost myself, remember? You're the only person capable of that, Lugh. I don't know what I'd do if you got captured or murdered."

I made that promise to a tearful Epona during our battle against the orc demon when she said she didn't want to fight anymore and that she was afraid of hurting other students and of forgetting herself.

"I know."

"I'd be mad if you didn't remember."

"I'd never do that to you, Epona."

That was the reason I was summoned to this world, after all. As her friend, I was doing all I could to prevent her from destroying the world. However, if my efforts failed, for the people

I loved, and for Epona herself—for the girl who cried because she didn't want to hurt anyone—I would kill her.

"All right, I'll see you later, Lugh." Epona walked off.

I watched her go and dropped my fake smile. "She's a good kid, but still too naive." I sighed and heard a loud *thud* behind me. The sound's origin was a slender man, gagged and bound with rope, hitting the floor.

Quiet footsteps approached from behind him.

"Wow, you were right, my lord. There actually was someone following you," said Tarte, who was wearing her uniform.

I'd asked Tarte to follow behind Epona and me to capture anyone she saw spying on us. Essentially, I'd asked her to tail the person tailing us. When pursuing someone, it was easy to focus too heavily on your target and leave yourself defenseless—although any spy who allowed that to happen was second-rate. Unfortunately for the guy tailing Epona and me, he was that incompetent, and Tarte easily captured him.

I observed the collapsed man. *Hmm. He's actually better than I gave him credit for.*

Looking at Tarte, I stated, "You've gotten stronger."

"Huh?" she responded in confusion.

"I see only one injury on the back of his head. That's proof that you rendered him helpless with a single blow, without him noticing your approach. This man is a professional, and you should be proud you succeeded against him. There aren't many in the world as talented as you are at your age," I explained.

Tarte caught the man because she was supremely adept, not because of any lack of proficiency on his part.

"N-no, I don't deserve that praise. You've just taught me a lot, my lord," Tarte denied.

"If that was all, you would not have come this far. You've worked very hard."

Even before I was told to retire and focus on teaching in my previous life, I had experience training many students. I taught many who had greater intuition than she did, but I never knew a student who grew as much as she had. It was a cliché, but hard work trumped genius when genius failed to work hard.

I patted her on the head, and she blushed and leaned into me. Despite her efforts to prevent it, her face softened into a smile. I found that side of her very cute. She was reluctant to part from me when I removed my hand.

"Let's deal with this guy," I said. The spy glared at me reproachfully. Tarte wasn't so foolish as to kill a source of information, so she left him alive.

I'd predicted that the hierarch would assign an observer to keep watch over me. He had no choice but to rely on Epona because she was the only person who could stop me, but she was also my friend. He must have considered the possibility that Epona would betray the church, and assigning an observer was a natural precaution—so natural that it was predictable.

"I taught you once in our classes about the dangers and practicalities of religion," I began.

"Yes, I remember. Fanatics abandon thought and become convinced that their religion is right about everything. They hear no arguments because they refuse to think for themselves. They are very useful as tools, but if you end up in conflict with them, you should consider them more beast than human," Tarte recounted.

"That's exactly right. The man you caught is one such zealot."

"Mmrgh, mmrrgh!"

The man struggled on the ground. He would never say that the Alamite Church had sent him. If a spy revealed their origins, it'd hurt their organization. There was no way he would allow that.

"How do you know that?" asked Tarte.

"His smell. The Alamite Church has a particular scent that is only given to followers who make vast donations or contribute greatly to their order in some other fashion. I smell it on this man," I explained.

The scent was originally thought up as a way to give followers a sense of superiority. Every religion used rank as part of the process of creating devout believers. The echelons were also made as simple to comprehend as possible.

That sense of superiority led people to become even more engrossed in the religion. Nothing stirred up loyalty within an organization like a feeling that you contributed more than anyone else, and that you were appreciated more than anyone else. I thought it likely that this man was given his special rank for his service rather than for his financial support.

Unfortunately for him, the church represented rank in the form of scent. A smell was excellent as an easily recognized badge, but no spy should've carried a sign that gave away their identity that easily.

"You're so smart, my lord! But if he's a fanatic, even letting him live won't get him to tell us anything... Should we just kill him, then? It would be bad if the church learned that Epona is supporting you, right? We could dispose of him easily enough using the furnace in the workshop you built at the academy," Tarte remarked casually.

"Mmrrggh, mmrrrrrrrggh, mrrggghh!"

The man began to struggle again after hearing such violent language from the lips of such a beautiful girl.

"I'm not going to do that. They'll think something happened if he disappears. Can you figure out what we should do here?" I challenged her.

A spy's disappearance was important information in and of itself.

"This is difficult. The best option would be to make him our friend, but he's not going to listen to us... Torturing won't work, either, because he'll take pride in suffering for the goddess. Sorry, I give up."

"I'll give you a sixty for that. Making him into our friend is the correct answer. He's going to give us some useful information."

"How are we going to do that if we can't win him over or torture him?"

"I want you to watch and learn. It's been a while since we've had this kind of lesson."

So far, my fight against the demons had involved very little of Tuatha Dé's secret profession. I hadn't gotten my hands dirty like this in quite some time. That said, I was a Tuatha Dé assassin by heart. There was no way I wouldn't put such great teaching material to use.

"Yes, my lord! I'll pay close attention!"

Tarte was not a genius. She was, however, a hard worker and obedient. I was confident she would continue to improve herself.

Okay, I have some preparation to do. As Tarte said, this man wouldn't listen to words and was prepared to endure any pain. This would be difficult playing by the book.

That was why I was going to use his body—more specifically,

the structure of his brain—against him. That was the difference between emotion and bodily reaction. There were certain parts of a person's biology you could use to get them to do anything. And by combining the magic of this world with the technology of my old one, the methods for doing so became all the more effective.

I did feel a little bad for the guy. But unfortunately for him, I was not so nice a person that I would go easy on the people trying to label me an enemy of the world and kill me in disgrace.

Carriages hauling the entirety of Class S and the students with the highest grades from Class A departed from the academy.

Officially, we were traveling to the Holy Land for Dia, Tarte, and me to be commended for our triumphs against the demons. The invitation had come directly from the Alamite Church and the Alam Karla, no less. Naturally, the students were excited.

Unfortunately, that's not the real reason for this trip. Thanks to the plot of the demon disguised as the hierarch, word was already circulating that I was a fraud who misappropriated the goddess's name. That was a serious crime. I would be treated as a criminal not just in Alvan, but in nearly every country on the continent.

They really should've acted more naturally if they wanted to keep that hidden from me, though, I thought with an involuntary laugh. I'd been separated from Dia and Tarte and placed between Epona and Naoise, the latter of whom was in league with a demon. Many of the strongest teachers at the academy were also in our carriage. Every precaution was taken to ensure I didn't run.

The reason they separated the three of us was not just to weaken me by removing my assistants but also to prevent us from trying anything. If one of us escaped alone, we wouldn't know what might become of the other two. In that way, we were all hostages.

"This is gonna be a long trip, Lugh. I've been in the capital this whole time, so I haven't ridden in a carriage for a while. It's nice," said Epona.

She was trying to make casual conversation, but her expression was strained. Epona had always been a bad actor. Actually, apart from her overwhelming strength, she was average or worse at most things. That lack of balance was actually typical of heroes.

"I'm the opposite. I've been racing all around the nation, so I'm sick of carriages," I responded.

Epona looked remorseful. "You've been giving your all to protect the kingdom in our place... I'm sorry, Lugh."

"No, I didn't mean it that way."

Epona reminded me of Tarte as she bowed her head in regret. Naoise looked at us and shrugged.

"I'm sick of the cowards in the capital only protecting themselves. They're letting the hero go to waste. I get chills thinking about where we'd be if Lugh wasn't around," he said.

The demon's goal was to create Fruits of Life and resurrect the Demon King. Ten thousand human souls were needed to form just one fruit. That made large cities likely targets, and because the government higher-ups feared that the capital would be attacked in the hero's absence, resulting in the loss of their lives or fortunes, they had anchored Epona to the city. Had she been able to move freely, I wouldn't have had to risk my life fighting demons.

That is exactly what is going to make things different this time around. According to the Alam Karla, the goddess said to the demon that "this hero is not being depleted enough." Normally, even if the rulers wanted to confine the hero to the capital, they'd have to be sent out to deal with demons because they were the only one who could. This time was different, however, because I was present.

I'd read all the literature I available, but I'd never found mention of a person other than the hero who had killed a demon.

"I'm fed up with them, too. I don't want anything to do with this 'Holy Knight' title," I agreed.

Naoise grinned. "Ha! That wouldn't sound genuine from anyone else, but you really don't care about stuff."

"I'll do something to convince those in power... I can't let you shoulder this burden alone, Lugh," said Epona.

I wanted the hero to join the fight, so I wasn't about to stop her. The only advantage to fighting the demons in Epona's place was gaining combat experience, and I'd been thinking lately that I'd acquired more than enough of that already.

We continued talking, our conversation turning fun and idle as if we were just three ordinary classmates. No one would have known we were a hero, a criminal, and the servant of a demon.

We made camp at night. Horses don't have good vision in darkness, and even though we got fresh horses at a town along the way, they needed rest. The carriages we were traveling in were sleeping carriages; they were spacious and had foldable bunk beds, so we could use them to sleep in overnight.

I wanted to know how Tarte and Dia were doing, but I didn't get permission when I tried to see them. I wasn't worried about them, though. Given the strength they had gained from My Loyal Knights, there were only two people in this camp who could harm them—Epona and Naoise—and those two were by my side.

Dia and Tarte might not be able to win if all the instructors worked together, but they would still be able to run. They were my assassination assistants, and I had spent more time training them in covert operations than I had in combat. Between strength and survival, the latter was more important.

I finished my meal, and just when I was about to return to the carriage to sleep because I had nothing else to do, Naoise grabbed my hand. "Want to go look at the stars? My domain is nearby, so I know a spot with a beautiful view."

The instructors watching me made startled expressions and readied themselves for action. Naoise settled them down with a glance.

"Yeah, that sounds nice. The sky will look different here than it does in Tuatha Dé," I answered.

The suggestion of stargazing was an excuse, of course. Naoise likely had something he could only talk to me about alone.

We arrived at the shore of a lake after a little walk. The reflection of the starry sky on the water's surface was beautiful.

Naoise smiled at me and put a finger to his lips. Seeing that, I performed a spell using a special vocalization technique without moving my lips. No one watching would have been able to tell that I had done anything.

The spell created a thin boundary around us that interrupted the flow of the air. Sound was the vibration of air, and by stopping that, I could stop sound. Naoise and I were essentially in an outdoor soundproof room. We were being watched by the instructors, but they wouldn't overhear us.

"We can say whatever we want now," I told him.

"That's a convenient spell. Could you teach it to me?" Naoise asked.

"You don't have the wind affinity, so it'd be impossible."

"That's disappointing."

The wind affinity had a great variety of uses. I chose all four basic affinities, but if I had to pick just one, I would've gone with wind.

"So, what did you take this risk to talk to me about?" I questioned.

"Yes, let's get right to it. This is a trap. The instructors are going to drug you and put you to sleep before we reach the Holy Land, and when we arrive, you're going to undergo a witch trial on the gallows," Naoise revealed.

"I figured as much. Sounds about right for a villain who has lied about his connection to the goddess."

Witch trials had occurred in this world as they had in my previous one. They resulted from a rumor that monsters were disguising themselves as humans and slipping into society. That a similar thing happened on two different planets said a lot about human nature. Suspicion made us lose our heads.

"...You knew that much already, huh?"

"Yep. Might as well tell you I also know that the hierarch is a demon."

"It doesn't appear as if Epona revealed this to you... I would really love to have you in my order of knights."

Naoise's order of knights was an organization he'd created to achieve his dream, and he only recruited young, talented people. My refusing his invitation led to Mina snaring Naoise with the temptation of greater power.

"My answer hasn't changed."

"And I know better than to ask again. You've risen so high. I couldn't hope to contain you in my order... Especially not as things are now."

"I see. Is that all you had to say?"

"No. I have some information for you. The nickname of the demon disguised as the hierarch is the 'Puppeteer.' Mistress Mina told me to tell you that."

"That's helpful... I haven't seen mention of anything like that in the books I've read."

"I can't say I'm surprised. It is a puppeteer, after all."

That nickname suggested that the demon had the ability to manipulate marionettes. It had likely always remained hidden and made his puppets do the fighting for him.

This reminded me of something I'd observed in the books I'd read. Of the eight demons, seven of them were depicted the same way in every era. One of them, however, was different every time, to the point that each iteration seemed like an entirely different individual. If this demon had powers that the nickname "Puppeteer" suggested, then that checked out. The demons depicted in literature were not the Puppeteer, but his dolls.

"Is that all the information you have?" I asked.

"Yeah, that's it. Did I disappoint you?" Naoise responded.

"No, that's enough. Not knowing that could have been lethal."

Being put on a witch trial was one of the things I'd expected. I had a plan for that scenario that involved killing the hierarch during the trial and using his regeneration ability to show everyone that he was a demon.

Demon regeneration was a compulsory and automatic process.

I used my fight with the orc demon to verify some theories. One of the things I'd tested was whether or not a demon would regenerate if its head was blown off. I wanted to see if regeneration depended on the brain, or if it bypassed thought altogether. My experiment proved that it was the latter.

If the hierarch regenerated after I blew off his head, everyone would realize it was a demon in disguise. However, if he was not a demon but a puppet, that changed everything. Killing him would make me a murderer, and I'd never regain my place in society.

"Mistress Mina will be delighted you said so. She said she wants to maintain a favorable relationship with you."

"That's good to hear. I'll play my part as well." At the very least, it seemed like Mina still intended to make use of me.

Finding out that the hierarch was a puppet took the strategy of killing him off the board. It also opened some new possibilities, however. I had to strategize to take advantage of them.

Killing the hierarch and making him regenerate hadn't been very high in my plans anyway. Truthfully, new tactics I devised this late wouldn't be my first options, either. They held too much risk. The best outcome would be for me to win the trial fair and square.

Even still, I was going to devote myself to working on fresh strategies. Any number of unexpected things could occur during an assassination. You needed to be scrupulous with backup plans. I polished each mentally, considering their chances of success, and compared them to my existing schemes to decide priority.

I need to fill Dia and Tarte in as well. We operated as a team, and there would be no point to my plans if I was the only one who knew them.

"Wanna head back, Naoise? It's getting cold out," I suggested.

He nodded. "Sure thing."

I was being kept isolated from Dia and Tarte, but conveying information to them wouldn't be hard. We had our radio communication devices, and they were the type that could send and receive broadcasts within two kilometers, even without a large terminal present. No one knew of radio correspondence, so we could use the tools in plain sight without issue.

I was going to check to see how they were doing and tell them about my new plans in detail.

Our carriages resumed travel early the next morning. Dia and Tarte told me that they were both placed on different wagons and that their camps were made hundreds of meters from mine. They were being watched, too, though not as heavily as me. It seemed that the instructors were under the impression that while we operated as a team, I was the only one who held special strength.

That said, the instructors had assigned a team of Class S upperclassmen to supervise Dia and Tarte. And Nevan was in charge.

So that's why Nevan gave me an immediate reply when I asked for her help.

Dia, Tarte, and I didn't have the power to overcome the demon's trap alone. With the three of us under constant observation, I needed someone who could act freely. It couldn't just be anyone, either; they had to understand the situation and still be willing to help.

Nevan was the only person I could think of who satisfied those conditions, but I'd expected that gaining her cooperation would be difficult. Upperclassmen at the Royal Academy were treated almost the same as active knights, meaning they were handed a variety of duties and spent a great amount of time away from campus. Nevan may have been a Romalung, but she couldn't ignore her responsibilities. Her authority as the daughter of a duke meant nothing at the academy.

She was able to accept my request in spite of that because her duties already took her to the Holy Land...to watch over Dia and Tarte. *Nevan acting as their chaperone suits us perfectly. Dia and Tarte will be able to fill her in on my plans.*

We were currently taking a lunch break, and circumstances were giving me a small headache.

Did they seriously think a Tuatha Dé wouldn't notice this amateurish method of poisoning?

The instructors had mixed sleeping medication and a muscle relaxant into my soup, but they were both the type that you could smell. Also, despite soup being a convenient food to make while camping, because you could prepare a large amount all at once, they had gone out of their way to cook mine in a separate smaller pot. It was as if they were crying out for me to suspect them.

If I was going to have Tarte poison somebody, I would choose a drug with little taste or smell and hide its presence by serving a broth with a strong taste and fragrance.

While stifling my astonishment, I ate a spoonful. I conjectured about the type of poison as I tasted it. My body had antibodies that resisted toxins because I'd been ingesting them since early childhood, and Rapid Recovery counteracted poison in no time. This caliber of drug was no problem.

However, if the poison didn't affect me, I could see the instructors resorting to violence to try to subdue me. Epona believed in my innocence, so I wasn't scared of whatever the instructors attempted, but her getting involved now would cause me problems down the line.

With that in mind, I guessed at the effects this poison would have on an ordinary person so I could act them out. After ten minutes, I'd pretend my body was growing heavy and my vision hazy. Then I'd become completely immobilized and fall asleep. The instructors bought it, restraining me without suspecting a thing or noticing I was feigning sleep.

They're using Sorcerer Cuffs, a tool for mage criminals. They're also giving me a stronger oral muscle relaxant, as if the bindings aren't enough.

Mages essentially always had a weapon, even when unarmed. All it took was a simple spell to break out of prison. That was why special precautions against mages had been developed. They were designed to diffuse mana and rendered even elite mages unable to cast magic. The instructors used three sets of them on me.

That may have sounded like a problem, but the cuffs weren't going to prevent me from using spells. Their effects were strong, but the scattered mana just drifted in the surrounding air. I'd used my Spell Weaver skill to develop many spells with Dia, and one of those counteracted Sorcerer Cuffs. Essentially, it gathered the mana scattered into the air and used it to break the anti-mage bindings.

I can break out of my restraints at any time. The problem right now is the muscle relaxant. The drug was nothing my poison immunities and Rapid Recovery couldn't handle. However, acting out the effects was going to be extremely challenging. *This strong of a drug would cause my bladder and sphincters to relax, which means I should be soiling myself. If I don't, they might realize the chemical isn't working.*

I wouldn't have hesitated to soil myself in my previous life. Now, though, I had no desire to do so. I didn't want Dia and Tarte to witness such a shameful sight.

Geez, becoming more human comes with its own host of problems.

In the end, I relieved myself like I needed to. Maintaining the facade was more critical than maintaining my ego. There was no explanation for not soiling myself after a drug like that. Fortunately, they immediately changed my pants and underwear, but that was humiliating in and of itself.

Funnily enough, the instructors began to leak information to me unwittingly as I pretended to be unconscious. I was to be handed to the church as soon as we reached the Holy Land, and my trial was scheduled to begin promptly. If I lost, I'd be executed. That was the way it should have been, anyhow. Considering the church's influence, my death and guilt had already been decided.

Not all of the instructors blindly believed the church, and some even thought it would be best to defend me. Yet as members of the military, they couldn't disobey orders. That was what motivated their actions.

So the pigs in the capital are following orders from the church and turning me in without question… Do they understand what this will mean? With me out of the picture, they won't be able to keep Epona at their doorstep. That was how scared they were of Alamism's leaders. It didn't feel good being discarded this easily after risking my life to kill demons.

I recalled words my dad had once told me. *"Tuatha Dé is the blade that cuts unhealthy presences out of the Alvanian Kingdom. We hold that pride in our hearts and do what we believe is right… But the country sees us as nothing more than expendable tools. If need be, they will cast us aside."*

I'd always understood that. That was what assassins were. No job could've been more thankless. The reason I still fought was to protect the Tuatha Dé domain. I wanted to protect the place where my parents, Dia, Tarte, and Maha lived. The place I had come to belong.

Even poor treatment like this would not cause me to waver in that conviction. The kingdom may have been trying to discard me, but I was still going to do what I had to.

For myself and the people I love, I will excise this tumor—this pest— that threatens this world.

I sharpened that feeling into a blade as the instructors relinquished me to the church. The members of the church who collected my body injected me with even more drugs, a psychotropic and an intoxicant, and forced me to drink a large amount of alcohol.

A normal person wouldn't have been able to hold a conversation. They would've been delirious and devoid of reason, perhaps even possessed. It was clear how poorly a person would fare in a witch trial in that condition.

This was probably standard procedure for the church. Its members employed methods to turn even the most virtuous person into an utter fool. And by ruining the credibility and achievements of the accused, the church spread the notion of its own righteousness.

I couldn't deny the tactic's efficacy. Unfortunately for them, however, drugs didn't work on me. I was going to face the inquisition in perfect condition.

A guillotine had been set up in the central plaza of the Holy Land, which had been chosen as the venue for my hearing. Five chairs had been arranged in a semicircle behind the guillotine, according to formal procedure, and five high-ranking members of the church in formal dress were sitting in them.

Those five people were acting as prosecutor, judge, and jury for this trial. The same group performing all three roles meant this tribunal was obviously flawed. To make matters worse, the audience was composed of Holy Land residents, all of whom were fervent believers of Alamism. They saw the quintet of church leaders presiding over this hearing as divine agents. I'd never seen such a terrible proceeding, even in my previous world.

I'd been dressed as a prisoner, three sets of Sorcerer Cuffs had been placed around my hands, and my head was fixed into the guillotine. This was less than ideal.

"The inquisition of the wicked criminal Lugh Tuatha Dé, who used the goddess's name for deception, will now commence!"

Hmm. They're calling it an inquisition instead of a witch trial. It made no difference. The demon thought it had already won. It was at least partially aware that I was responsible for the Alam Karla's abduction. And it believed that by restricting Dia, Tarte, and me from action, it would prevent me from using that to my advantage.

I was going to penetrate the chinks in the demon's armor and kill it. That was how assassins operated.

Passionate cheers sounded from every direction as the audience called for my punishment.

I observed the situation around me. Dia and Tarte were under surveillance, but they were in position. Nevan was with a hooded girl. She gave me the sign. Events were proceeding according to plan.

The hierarch was a slender man in his sixties with all the presence appropriate for his position. Upon closer inspection, however, I saw that his eyes were devoid of emotion. Even more surprisingly, my Tuatha Dé eyes, which could see mana, revealed that there were strings of magic power attached to his heart, as if he were a puppet. That led to one more discovery: All the hierarch's mana was streaming into him from those threads.

It was widely believed that non-mages didn't have mana, but that was incorrect. Even non-mages produced a tiny amount by nature of being alive. That applied to all living creatures, not just humans. Despite that, the hierarch produced none at all.

He's already dead... That was why this demon was called the Puppeteer. His power only allowed him to manipulate dolls, not living creatures. Logically, it would have been best to keep the hierarch alive. That the demon was manipulating his corpse must have meant that his ability could not be used on the living. This confirmed for me that the information Mina gave me was true.

"Hear his crimes! Lugh Tuatha Dé has spread the dangerous falsehood that he was chosen by the goddess! This insolent behavior cannot be allowed to continue!" the hierarch declared.

The calls to punish me grew even louder. They weren't chanting for my death; this was the center of the world's religion, and people were too well-behaved for that. My disciplining was a guillotine to the neck, though, so it wasn't like there was much difference.

"We have proof of his misdeeds! The Alam Karla, oracle of the goddess, has bestowed the following divine message: 'Punish the false Holy Knight!' If you have a defense, Lugh Tuatha Dé, speak it now," the hierarch continued.

The demon had multiple reasons for going to such great lengths. The first was to eliminate me, as I'd been snowballing into a bigger threat to the demons than the hero was. Exhausting Epona was the second. The demon disguised as the hierarch—the Puppeteer—expected me to resist once it looked like I was about to be executed. If I did so, it would be the hero's job to stop me. The plan would simultaneously eliminate an enemy of the demons and weaken Epona, who hadn't been depleted at all, because I'd been fighting in her place. It took out two birds with one stone.

That was why I needed to undermine the Puppeteer's assumptions. Fortunately, Epona was my friend, and she believed me over the hierarch.

I chose to live as a human in this life, and while searching for a path that doesn't involve killing Epona, I ended up becoming her friend... And now that relationship is proving fortunate.

Had I only ever considered Epona as a target to kill and kept her at a distance, she probably would have done as the hierarch ordered and fought me.

I had one more supposition to tear down as well. To do so, I needed to end this absurd witch trial. The demon believed that I couldn't properly defend myself because of the overmedication. I'd been acting like the drugs were affecting me to deceive everyone. Creeping up on a target from a blind spot and catching them off guard was standard practice for an assassin. Sometimes, instead of waiting for an opening, you had to make one yourself.

It was time to unveil the results of all my preparation.

"Might of Heaven!"

I blasted the three pairs of Sorcerer Cuffs off my hands using Might of Heaven, which gathered the mana scattered in the air by the Sorcerer Cuffs to perform a spell. With mana now filling my body, my restraints could no longer hold me. I tore myself out of my chains, forced my head out of the guillotine, and rolled my shoulders to get loose.

"Guards! Seize the criminal!" the hierarch commanded.

Six guards charged at me simultaneously. They were only ordinary humans. They moved in sync and looked relatively skilled, but they were no match for me. I dodged them, then gently dislocated their joints to immobilize them. In just a few seconds, I was the only one left standing. Everyone present was amazed by my masterful skill.

I raised my hands and addressed the hierarch. "Don't get the wrong idea. I have no intention of running from this witch trial... or inquisition, as you call it. I merely removed these impediments to make it easier to speak."

"How did you remove those Sorcerer Cuffs?!" the hierarch screamed.

I smiled boldly in response and cast a wind spell. It was very simple magic that did nothing but amplify my voice, but I had a

specific reason for using it. The volume of your voice could be a huge advantage when appealing to the hearts of an audience. I also changed the quality of my voice slightly to make it resonate better and impart a more sincere impression.

Many people underestimated what was required to make an effective speech. It took far more than the words alone. Delivering an address meant putting on a performance and advocating to your crowd. The speaker needed to use gestures, the tone and volume of their voice, intonation, appearance, and more to win over the onlookers.

"A miracle of the goddess. She saved me and cleared my body of the drugs you forced into me as well," I responded for all to hear. A murmur rose from the people.

The hierarch and the other high priests sitting next to him began to scream. Unfortunately for them, however, while their cries reached me, they did not reach the audience. There was no way natural voices could be heard by this large a crowd when every person in it was talking, even if they were doing so at a whisper.

The priests were my judges, so winning the hearing itself was an impossibility. As a result, I went in aiming for a different victory condition—winning the hearts of the masses.

I ignored the shrieking priests and continued talking. The key to my victory was earning the people's support, so the best thing for me to do was amplify my voice further and drown out the priests.

"The goddess chose me and bestowed a means with which to defeat demons! I have obeyed her wishes and killed three of them! No ordinary human is capable of such deeds! I have achieved what I have because of the goddess's blessing!"

The discourse among the throng grew. I could hear some voices; hearts were wavering. No matter what the hierarch accused me of, he couldn't erase my accomplishments. There was also no explanation, save divine intervention, for how someone other than the hero could kill demons.

It wasn't going to be that easy, though. The weight of the hierarch's authority as the highest pillar of Alamism still held ground, and few people actually trusted my assertion. The audience had been confident of my crimes earlier, and now the dominating mood was confusion. That meant it was time to play my card.

I gave the signal, and few among the crowd responded.

This is where the real game begins.

I surveyed my surroundings as I thought things over. I'd prepared a variety of plans beforehand. The question was which to use. The most important factor in my decision was the audience's mood.

My social standing hung in the balance, so I couldn't afford a mistake. It wouldn't be hard to give up the name of Lugh Tuatha Dé and live as a different person. I was already prepared to do so, because assassins could be discarded by their employers at any time.

I didn't want to choose that option if it could be avoided, however. I loved my life as Lugh Tuatha Dé, the people I shared it with, and the Tuatha Dé domain. That was why I had to win this trial and absolve myself.

"You make me laugh, criminal. You say it was the goddess's power that freed you from those shackles?! Ha! That only proves that you are a devil!" the hierarch declared.

Somehow, his voice was just as loud as my spell-amplified one. Were he using magic, my Tuatha Dé eyes would have seen the flow of mana.

I observed attentively and realized how he was doing it. He was simply yelling. The Puppeteer had removed the limiter on the hierarch's brain, enabling him to yell so loudly that he damaged his throat. The demon could ignore the limits in place to protect the body because the hierarch was a lifeless doll. This made it impossible for me to make sure the crowd only heard what I had to say, but I didn't really mind that.

"Answer me this. Why would a devil kill demons? Why would a devil save human lives?" I challenged.

"I will not listen to the prattling of a wicked creature! Hero Epona, slay this unholy criminal right this instant!" the hierarch commanded, shifting his eyes to Epona, who was standing by the scaffold.

Placing her close by was a natural precaution. They knew that if I somehow broke out of my restraints, she would be the only one who could stop me. It'd be a simple task for her.

However...

"He's never felt like a devil to me... I want to hear what Lugh has to say. This is a trial, not an execution, isn't it?"

...Epona trusted me. The hierarch—or rather, the Puppeteer—had made a miscalculation. It was ignorant of the friendship the hero and I shared.

"I know it to be true! I am the hierarch of the Alamite Church, and I can see the devil attached to this criminal! He must be executed!"

"You still haven't answered my last question. If I'm a devil, why would I kill demons and rescue the enemy? People lie, but actions do not," I countered.

"Listen, all! Do not let this dark one's sweet-talk lead you astray!"

The hierarch had no argument. He hadn't given a single answer to my question. Typically, crowds detested this kind of evasion, but unfortunately, that wasn't the case this time.

This is *the seat of Alamism, after all... Having deep faith sounds*

like a good thing, but they've been brainwashed into abandoning individ-
ual thought. They completely trust that I'm the devil the hierarch brands
me as.

They believed a groundless accusation over my logical argument, and all because it came from the hierarch. I'd predicted
things would turn out this way, but I didn't think it would be this
bad. Nothing I said now would accomplish anything.

I'll have to turn the tables, then. To get these believers to listen, I
need greater authority than the hierarch.

I made a previously agreed-upon sign toward the audience.
Neither Dia nor Tarte was its recipient. The church knew that they
were my allies, thus they were under surveillance and couldn't
do anything too bold. Obviously, the girls could shake off those
watching them, but that would make the enemy needlessly wary.

My signal was meant for Nevan. There was a girl next to her
with a hood over her eyes. Nevan grabbed her hand and forced
her way toward the stage.

There were many guards around the platform, but they had
no hope of stopping the greatest masterpiece of humanity. Nevan
dealt with them as easily as she would have with children, despite
the handicap of leading a girl behind her.

There was a beautiful, balletic quality to Nevan's movements.
She sent every guard she touched flying into the air as though they
weighed nothing at all, each one getting concussed and knocked
out when they hit the ground. What she did took great skill. Even
in her disadvantageous position, she was able to incapacitate all
who obstructed her without injuring them. And that wasn't even
the most surprising thing about this.

I can't believe the daughter of a duke would do something this risky...
All I'd asked Nevan to do was bring the girl to me. Undoubtedly,

she was clever enough to find a way to accomplish that without standing out much. That she didn't make an effort to conceal her identity spoke to her trust in me. She was also putting on a performance to give the next phase of our plan more of an impact.

The high priests sat dumbfounded in their chairs for a moment. When they regained their wits, they each went scarlet in the face and began to hurl insults at Nevan.

"Have you lost your mind?!"

"Don't think your status as a member of one of the four major dukedoms will let you get away with this!"

"The Alamite Church speaks for the goddess. Opposing us is the same as rebelling against the goddess herself!"

People are taught from an early age that the high priests speak for the goddess. Anyone else on this continent would've prostrated themselves before the holy officials and begged for forgiveness after weathering the verbal tirade that Nevan just had. She displayed no interest in doing so, however. With a smile, she gracefully brushed her hair aside.

"I fail to understand what you mean. I'm acting against the goddess? There has been a terrible misunderstanding. I'm here *for* the goddess," Nevan replied.

"How could that violence have possibly been for the goddess?! Leave us immediately. We will get to your punishment later... Actually, if you capture this criminal for us, we will forgive your sins. The goddess's mercy knows no bounds!"

Hmm... They're acting tough, but they're clearly afraid of me without my restraints. That was understandable. If Epona refused to intervene, then no one could stop me. Nevan's strength, the excellence of the Romalung bloodline, was known far and wide beyond

Alvan. Perhaps the high priests believed she stood a chance against me.

"I have been curious about something for quite some time. Why do ordinary humans like you pretend to be spokespeople of the goddess? That is blasphemy," Nevan accused.

"We are high priests of the Alamite Church. Our deep understanding of the goddess's will allows us to speak for her," the hierarch shot back. The audience cheered at his words.

"There is no reality to that claim. I will have nothing to do with it. After all, I'm here on true orders from the goddess... Isn't that right, Your Holiness?"

The girl next to Nevan threw back her hood, revealing snow-white hair and artificially whitened skin modeled after the goddess's.

"I am the Alam Karla. I..."

The girl I'd asked Nevan to deliver to me was the Alam Karla herself. I'd requested Nevan collect her from the safe house and bring her here.

My argument wasn't reaching the audience. The people believed that the hierarch spoke for the divine, leaving my assertions as nothing but devilish trickery. As long as the crowd believed that, nothing I said would reach them.

That meant I needed to change their minds about the hierarch. The words of the Alam Karla, the true oracle of the goddess, held more weight than anything some greedy old man who held nothing more than an earthly position said. The Alam Karla would be able to wash away the demon's accusation and give me even ground on which to win the trial with logic. That was my plan.

My victory was all but assured the moment Nevan brought

the Alam Karla onto the stage. Yet suddenly, my sixth sense went off.

Something invisible penetrated my body. It took root inside me, and I lost all bodily sensation.

"*Refine. Process.*"

Before I knew it, I was using earth magic. I produced metal and then shaped it into a knife. These were signature spells of mine.

My body was acting against my will. *Puppeteer...* The word flashed in the back of my mind.

This was impossible. It didn't make any sense. I saw the threads connected to the hierarch with my Tuatha Dé eyes. Upon discovering that the demon manipulated his puppets using mana strings, I exercised maximum caution to ensure that the same wouldn't happen to Epona or me. But somehow, the demon had gotten its hooks into me without my noticing.

I'd fallen right into the demon's trap... The Puppeteer was capable of creating invisible strings but had intentionally made those connected to the hierarch visible to give me the mistaken impression that I'd always be able to see them. I understood now why Mina was wary of the remaining demons. They truly were special.

I couldn't stop my feet from moving, nor resist the demon's control. I raised the knife I'd just created and turned my refined assassin's techniques upon the Alam Karla to take her head.

Ah, I see. This is why the church didn't take action, even though it knew that the Alam Karla had been abducted. The Puppeteer had predicted that I would bring the Alam Karla here. It might have even known about the friendship Epona and I shared. That was entirely possible if Mina had passed her fellow demon information on me in the same way she'd given me intel on the Puppeteer. Naoise knew of my friendship with Epona. Perhaps he'd sold me out.

The Puppeteer let the Alam Karla escape so it could take control of me and force me to kill her in front of this large crowd. This plan allowed the demon to slay the disobedient oracle and easily install a suitable replacement. It also spelled my certain ruin. Epona would have no choice but to kill me, and she would even be depleted in our fight.

The demon was killing three birds with one stone. In just a few seconds, my knife was going to cut off the Alam Karla's head.

I clenched my teeth.

A smile formed on my face.

Ever since I heard the name "Puppeteer," I'd been half-expecting this to occur. I'd also been growing more and more suspicious because of the church's lack of action after the abduction of the Alam Karla. Furthermore, given the demon's nickname, I knew that getting caught off guard and made into a marionette was a possibility. I was prepared for this.

The third arm attached to my shoulder exposed itself by tearing through my clothes. It was a divine treasure, a god limb I'd stolen from the noble who tried to bring me down. The arm performed a sweep above my head. I regained freedom of movement immediately, then put away the knife and brought myself to a stop.

I was finally able to put this divine treasure to use. The god arm's distinct ability was that it could touch things that otherwise could not be touched. Mana, souls, miasma, spirits—nothing was out of reach.

I'd performed special preparations on the god arm beforehand. I set it up so that if I ever stopped sending a cancellation code at regular intervals, it would act to break off everything that had been fastened to me. The scariest thing about being controlled was that you were incapable of resisting via normal means. That was why I'd set the arm to activate if I didn't transmit the code.

Getting the arm here was a lot of trouble. It was small enough to hide under loose clothing, but it was still a metal arm. The church officials guarding me would've confiscated it before bringing me to trial. To keep it hidden, I'd stored it in my Leather Crane Bag and then hidden that in my stomach. I'd retrieved the bag and the arm after the body search and attached the latter when no one was looking.

Carrying hidden weapons was one of the fundamentals of being an assassin. Human bodies had more hiding places than you'd expect, and the stomach was one of the most popular ones.

You amateurs, it's standard practice to check inside the stomach and the anus. Were I to perform a body search, I'd do that much at least.

Now free from danger, the Alam Karla took a deep breath and faced the crowd.

"Hear my words. The hierarch is under the control of a demon. He was about to kill me before Lugh Tuatha Dé saved me on guidance from the goddess, and I have been in hiding ever since. I, the Alam Karla, swear to you that Lugh Tuatha Dé was chosen by the goddess."

The mood of the crowd shifted instantaneously. The eyes on me turned from loathing to envy with startling speed. I heard voices saying things like, "Oh, I see" and "So that's what happened." They were recalling the rumor I'd spread about the message the Alam Karla left in lipstick on the day I'd abducted her. I'd manipulated the discussion around her disappearance with this moment in mind.

"I have one more declaration to make. With Epona, the goddess's hero, and Lugh, who has received the goddess's divine guidance, both present, now is the time to root out the demon who has contaminated the church!"

I didn't know the Alam Karla to be the type who could deliver a line like that off the top of her head in such a tense situation. It wasn't in the script I'd written beforehand. Perhaps Nevan put it into Myrrha's head. The masterpiece of House Romalung never failed to impress. She'd anticipated the audience's reaction and altered the preset speech to better suit the circumstances. I almost couldn't stand how gifted she was.

The high priests lost themselves to fury, screaming and shouting at us without a hint of reason or dignity, sounding more animal than human. The crowd watched them with cold eyes. The Alam Karla had stripped them of their authority. Now, the people could see the holy officials for who they really were—ranting, repulsive, middle-aged men who abused their power.

Among them, the hierarch alone stood calm and quiet. His blank face resembled a dropped doll's. When he finally spoke, he remained expressionless. His inhuman demeanor suggested that the demon realized there was no longer any point in acting.

"Awww, I failed. That's too bad. Was it a favorable alteration of fate by the goddess that brought you that godly toy, or was it mere coincidence? Ah, I was so close."

His tone sounded like that of a childish adult.

"I would've managed even without Airgetlam," I responded.

That wasn't a boast. Having the god arm enabled me to execute a plan where it didn't matter if the demon caught me off guard and took control of me. Had I not possessed the divine treasure, I would've opted for a strategy that guaranteed that the Puppeteer never hijacked my body in the first place.

"I understand now. You're clever because you're weak. Humans lack the strength of monsters, so you must rely on cunning if you wish to overcome the limitations of your species and challenge us. That means physical strength is not the only kind of might. This is useful information."

As soon as the demon finished speaking, the hierarch charged with teetering, mechanical movements and impossible speed. I could hear his muscles snapping, and I saw an overload of magical power shorting his mana circuits, yet the demon ignored them and forced the hierarch at me. His mouth opened so wide to bite me that his jaw separated from his skull.

No matter how swift the attack, I was too experienced to allow an attack like that to connect. I twisted my body, and the hierarch fell face-first onto the ground, his head penetrating the earth and getting stuck. What absurd strength.

While astonished at the sight, I used an earth spell to turn dirt into iron. I was fighting a puppet, which meant death was not enough to win. That's why I was burying the hierarch alive in iron. That would prevent him from moving.

Although the hierarch was taken care of, I couldn't relax yet. This demon was the Puppeteer, after all, and he had an enormous supply of potential marionettes at his disposal.

"Tch, it's started."

Countless strings appeared from somewhere unseen. Some of them came my way, and I grabbed Nevan and dodged. I was able to evade the threads because I saw mana with my Tuatha Dé eyes. Mana was invisible, meaning only I saw the mana-woven strings.

"...He got fifty-seven people," I observed.

Puppet strings had been tied to fifty-seven individuals in the crowd. Every one of them stared at me with inhuman expressions.

They immediately sprinted for me, throwing aside those in front of them.

...*What should I do here?* Killing them would be easy. They were innocent people, though, and I didn't want their deaths on my conscience. It wasn't like ending their lives would accomplish much anyway. The Puppeteer would just connect its strings to other people in the crowd.

We wouldn't get anywhere until we cut off the source, but the Puppeteer had hidden somewhere. Given the demon's fighting style, there was no reason for it to show itself.

"This was the one plan I didn't want to use," I said, scratching my head.

This situation was the fourth worst scenario. The absolute worst was the demon taking control of Epona. The reason it hadn't done so was because it couldn't. Epona had a treasure trove of skills, and one of those must have rendered the threads ineffective. That was a natural conclusion—if the Puppeteer had been able to take control of Epona, it would have just summoned her with the hierarch and taken control of her instead of going through all this trouble to set a trap.

I was extremely grateful for that. I didn't want any part of fighting Epona.

"Epona, subdue all the people under the demon's control without killing them. It's impossible for me, but you can do it," I instructed.

Incapacitating living puppets without slaying them couldn't be achieved without overwhelming strength. Injuring the affected people did nothing to stop them from moving. I could handle one or two, but fifty-seven at once was well beyond my capabilities.

"What are you going to do, Lugh?" Epona asked.

"Kill the demon. I can find him by following his strings. I'm the right one for the job, just like you are for protecting these people," I explained.

"Okay, sounds good. You can leave the crowd to me."

Thank goodness Epona was here. I would've had to kill all these innocents if not for her. Unfortunately, leaving her here to save them meant that she would be unable to fight the demon. If the demon opted for this tactic because it was aware of my preference not to harm victims, it was truly dangerous.

"This is the final act. Listen well, Puppeteer. I'm going to sneak up on you and take your head like the assassin I am."

After that declaration of war, I took off running.

Screams and bellows rang out from all over. Ordinary people were suddenly rampaging and attacking all in their way. It was a terrifying environment.

I wish I could just run like they are...

Despite being the ones to put on this excessive witch trial, the high priests fled as quickly as they could. They excelled at self-preservation. Not that I could blame them. Escape was preferable to remaining here.

"Dia, Tarte! Pattern C-7!" I yelled loudly enough for them to hear me in the midst of the panicked crowd. Pattern C-7 meant that I was going to take on the demon alone, and that they were to focus on rescuing people. I watched them get to work, then jumped up high and rode the wind to remain airborne.

"I have a clear view from up here."

The Puppeteer's greatest weakness was that it could not control people without the mana threads. What made the demon so fearsome was that it could produce an endless amount of easily replaceable soldiers, all while remaining hidden. However, those strings still led right to him.

I focused mana into my Tuatha Dé eyes to strengthen my vision and ability to see mana. I had to count myself lucky that he wasn't using the invisible strings that caught me off guard earlier... That would've made this really difficult. *I'll be in trouble if I don't hurry.* My shoulders were burning. Pain racked my entire body, centered on where I'd affixed the Airgetlam. It may have been a divine treasure, but installing a foreign object on my body naturally came with adverse effects.

I couldn't afford to take it off, though. I couldn't defend myself against the invisible strings. Without the arm, I would be finished the next time they got me.

"There it is."

I accelerated using wind thrusters. The strings led to a totally plain house—an ideal hiding place that would never draw suspicion.

I felt someone watching me through a window. I sped up more and kicked through the pane, only to be greeted by countless strings that I had no hope of avoiding. Dodging them was impossible, so I charged forward instead. The threads penetrated my body, stealing the freedom of movement, but as soon as the god arm stopped receiving the cancellation code, it swiped and cut me free.

Once I regained control, I drew a large knife of a new variety that I'd developed, and with the momentum that carried me crashing through the window, I used the blade to cut open an overly thin, gray-skinned man. The regeneration ability unique to demons activated immediately, but the wound healed slowly, and he continued to bleed.

"This is problematic. I see the god arm wasn't your only trump card," the demon commented. His way of speaking sounded intellectual, almost like that of a scientist. That and his human appearance would've made it difficult to recognize him as a demon had I not already known.

"That's right. I have plenty of others ready as well," I replied.

I'd fought several demons already, and one thing always left me feeling uneasy. Unless I manifested a Crimson Heart using Demonkiller and destroyed it, the demon would restore itself immediately, no matter how I wounded them. That placed me in a very disadvantageous position and greatly limited my options in battle. If the demons were sharing information, my battle strategy would eventually cease working on them. After all, Demonkiller was a flawed spell and complicated to use.

"Hmm, that blade was made from the fangs of one of my brethren. How cruel of you."

"If demons can kill each other, I hypothesized that a piece of a demon's body could injure another of its kind... It looks like I was right."

I'd crafted this knife using one of the lion demon's fangs. It was made of strange material that was hard and sharp enough to bite through mithril armor, yet also resistant to impact, so I'd decided to collect it from the demon's corpse.

Being made from a demon gave the knife capability beyond that of a mere strong weapon. There were numerous accounts in literature of demons fighting each other, and even some cases where one of them was said to have died. That meant that demons could slay each other. Previously, it had only been a theory, but I'd just proved it correct.

The Puppeteer sent strings at me. I dodged them by a paper-thin margin, dropped low, accelerated abruptly to vanish from the demon's view, and took one soundless step to get behind him at a diagonal angle. Doing so made it appear to my opponent as though I'd vanished. This was an assassin's technique to catch people off guard at close range.

I stabbed the demon fang knife into the Puppeteer's neck and twisted my wrist to expand the wound. Purple blood erupted from his neck in a fountain.

"Hahhh, you are quite irritating, human," the demon stated calmly. He held his injury, then jumped away and broke through the wall behind him. Puppets charged through the hole. He'd evidently hidden his guards in a different room.

Unlike the hierarch, who was a manipulated corpse, these people were still alive. Because I was determined to avoid needless killing, living puppets were significantly more troublesome for me to deal with. Knocking them unconscious accomplished nothing, and immobilizing them without taking their lives was extremely difficult.

While bearing intense pain, I took manual control of the god arm, cut the strings attached to the puppets, and charged forward. This was the perfect opportunity to try one more experiment. I drew a gun from my holster. It was my standard one, but the bullets were special.

I took aim and fired six times, emptying the magazine instantly. The bullets glowed red as they flew through the air, and they all connected and wedged into the demon's flesh. *What's going to happen here?* I wondered. If this test succeeded, then fighting demons would become much easier.

"*Gah...* Hahhhh, hahhhhh. Impossible... These are...*khhk!*" the demon gasped out between coughs.

The bullets took effect immediately. The result was even greater than the knife's. No regeneration occurred at all. He looked no different than the thousands of humans I had shot across both of my lives.

"That's right. These are projectiles made from a demon's heart," I declared.

If demons could kill each other, that got me wondering if the most integral part of the demon, the collection of their power, might also work as their greatest poison. I'd saved all the Crimson Hearts we'd shattered so far and analyzed them from a variety of angles.

This time I decided to use the Crimson Hearts to create bullets. I made them into hollow point rounds, which penetrated less than ordinary bullets. Hollow point bullets were made distinct by their empty tips. When one hit a soft target, the hollow section burst and caused the tip to expand, inflicting massive internal damage. They didn't puncture well compared to other bullets, but they were very lethal and possessed excellent stopping power. This made them extremely useful for spreading poison throughout a body, as I was doing now.

"Hmm, this is what makes humans so frightening. From your weakness comes guile."

The Puppeteer was on the verge of death from blood loss. His essential organs had been damaged by the expanded hollow point bullets lodged in his body, leaving him immobilized. I could have left him to die on his own. He was a demon, though, so nothing would have surprised me. I was going to make sure I killed him.

"Why don't we talk this out, human? If you join forces with me, you could become the king of your kind... Oh, come now, you have nothing to worry about. Demons never betray another. We are much more trustworthy than humans," the Puppeteer said.

I didn't listen to him. I didn't even respond. His skill of

manipulation was too dangerous. If I took him up on that offer, all the people in my life could become his puppets before I knew it. His personality and trustworthiness were irrelevant; his very existence carried way too great a risk.

"You are clever, and cruel as well. More so than any monster—excuse me, hero—there has ever been."

I loaded new bullets into the revolver, then fired them all without any hesitation. The Puppeteer went completely motionless.

"I successfully killed him without using Demonkiller... But I need to monitor him for at least twenty-four hours to be absolutely certain he won't regenerate. The Holy Land likely has demon statues, so I'll have someone take a look at those as well."

I had to ensure the Crimson Heart bullets truly disabled the demon's regeneration. After taking a seat in a chair, I pulled out my radio communication device to report that I'd killed the demon and to ask Dia and Tarte to see if the corresponding statue was broken.

All right, this case is closed... Actually, not quite. I had a really annoying talk with the high priests awaiting me. I was sure all suspicion of me had been cleared, but merely imagining the ridiculous things they would say to save face put me in a foul mood.

The meeting was just as infuriating as I'd anticipated. Actually, it went beyond my expectations.

The high priests were lined up in front of me.

"Hmm, let's say that we were also under the control of that Puppeteer demon."

"That's a great idea. That alone makes us sound rather pathetic, though. We need something more."

"Then how about this? We ended up under his control in the end, but only after exhausting the demon's power with our heroic resistance. Without us, the demon never would have been killed."

"Oooh, I like it. That will preserve our reputations. You've done it again, Lord Storio."

They continued on like that forever. I almost respected how terrible it was. The person they tried to kill under false charges was right in front of them. However, they obviously didn't care as they shamelessly devised a cover story, their every word oozing with personal ambition and a desire for self-preservation. Dia was sitting next to me, and I laughed when I saw her hand move toward the holster on her thigh. I felt the same way.

Ultimately, the high priests settled on claiming they were victims of the Puppeteer. The headmaster of the academy rejected the nonsense about them weakening the demon. Although the high priests were unhappy about that, they reluctantly complied after being warned that excessive lying would make it more likely for someone to discover the truth.

As I walked through town the next day, I was serenaded with words and cheers of gratitude. Dia looked disgusted.

"Talk about two-faced. They were all screaming 'Die!' and 'Devil!' when you were on the platform, and now they're suddenly treating you like a living legend."

"I can't believe it, either. I think I'd feel guilty if I were in their place," Tarte agreed, evidently just as upset as Dia.

"I'm fine with it. I'm just glad they changed their minds," I responded.

It was human nature to despise admitting you were wrong. If a person threw stones at another, they would always be reluctant to think of their victim as anything other than a villain. That these people changed their minds about me so quickly made them impressive compared to the rest of humanity.

"I guess so... I just don't understand how they can go from a witch trial to praising you ceaselessly in two days," Dia complained.

"Things are much simpler this way. They've already forgotten about the false charges. They're even holding large celebrations. You see this kind of thing all the time. Countries that lose a war will often lift the gloomy feeling over the nation by celebrating individuals who gave distinguished service," I explained.

Human behavior didn't differ much between this world and

my old one. People were forgetful creatures, and unpleasant things could easily be swept under the rug by new events.

"Anyway, I am so relieved that your name was cleared, my lord," Tarte said.

"Yeah, I was ready to follow you anywhere, but I would really hate it if you couldn't be Lugh anymore," Dia concurred.

"Maha told me she would've been okay with you becoming Illig and staying by her side all the time, though," Tarte shared.

Maha said that, did she? It was likely because of how lonely she was living apart from me. Since we were engaged, I needed to make a better effort to spend time with her in the future.

"I'm not sure how to feel about you defeating the demon by yourself this time. Working together against the other ones was really hard, but it made me kind of happy, too," Dia admitted. Tarte nodded from her spot beside me.

Up until now, our basic strategy had been for Tarte to immobilize the demon, then for Dia to fire Demonkiller, then for me to finish the job. My new discoveries gave us more options.

"This time was an exception. I beat the Puppeteer alone because he relied on a special skill and wasn't particularly strong himself. Most of the demons aren't like that," I replied.

The orc demon was geared toward operating as a military commander, but the other demons we'd fought together all possessed tremendous individual strength. That trend indicated that most demons would be similar. Even with the demon fang knife and the Crimson Heart bullets, I didn't think I would've had much chance against the beetle, lion, or earth dragon alone.

Tarte sighed. "That's a relief. I feel uneasy sometimes at your ability to do everything on your own. It makes me wonder if you really need me."

"Right? You need to have *some* shortcomings, Lugh!" Dia appended.

The girls seemed to be bonding over that notion, but I didn't appreciate their wording. They had it all wrong.

"I can't do anything alone. I only manage because I have you both at my side," I explained.

"Do you really mean that?" Dia questioned.

"Of course."

"Heh-heh. I guess I've got no choice but to stick around, then. You're hopeless without me, after all." Dia hummed cheerfully, linking her arm with one of mine.

Tarte followed her example, hesitantly taking my other arm. "Um, I'm also happy to hear that you need me, my lord. I—I would not be able to live without you."

Dia nodded. "Me either. It was only for a few days, but being apart from you made me so lonely, angry, and sad that I felt like I was going to lose my mind."

"We must stay together forever... I almost seriously considered stabbing those watching me in my carriage while they were sleeping so that I could chase after you, my lord...," Tarte confessed.

"Coming from her, that's definitely no joke," Dia said.

It made me really happy to know how much the girls cared. It was a little embarrassing hearing how highly they thought of me, however. These last few days had been very trying for me, too. Being alone had been a natural part of my old life, but now it was unbearable.

That was a weakness. For an assassin, having loved ones was something others could take advantage of. By an assassin's logic, the majority of my actions were foolish and irrational. Still, I could definitively say that there was nothing wrong with the life I led as Lugh Tuatha Dé.

"Of the remaining three demons, Mina does not intend to destroy humanity. If we can kill the other two, we'll have peace," I stated.

"It feels like we're nearing the end." Dia grinned.

"I'll continue to work as hard as I can! I know we can do it!" exclaimed Tarte.

"Right. Let's see this to its conclusion."

If we could kill all the demons, prevent the resurrection of the Demon King, and stop Epona from turning on humanity, this world would survive, and my life could go on. I now had a visual of the goal that had initially seemed preposterously distant, and that included not killing the hero, who was my friend.

Why, then, was my assassin's sixth sense, trained over many decades to give me a feeling for impending danger, telling me that I was overlooking something?

Afterword

Thank you very much for reading *The World's Finest Assassin Gets Reincarnated in Another World as an Aristocrat*, Vol. 6. I am the author, Rui Tsukiyo.

In this volume, characters from the academy appeared again for the first time in a while. However, I think an even greater highlight was the advancement in Lugh's relationship with the heroines!

The next volume will finally touch on the primary mission of assassinating the hero. Please look forward to it!

Lastly, this series will be adapted into an anime. Please wait for further news!

Promotion

Redo of Healer, another one of my series that Kadokawa Sneaker Bunko is publishing, has an anime adaptation that began airing in January. Those unable to watch can find it on streaming sites such as Docomo Anime Store, so please check it out! It's a very lewd and harsh story, so it won't be for everyone, but those who like it will get hooked!

Thanks

Reia, as always, thank you for your wonderful illustrations!

I would also like to extend my deep gratitude to the lead editor and everyone else involved at Kadokawa Sneaker Bunko, Lead Designer Takahisa Atsuji, and all who have read this far! Thank you very much!

Celebrating the Anime Adaptation

Congratulations!!

I'm so happy we'll get to see everyone. I'm motional!!!! Thank you to everyone who has supported us!!